Sergeant Mags turned down a chance at a desk job to go out with into space and join others in discovering the answers on a different world. She was more interested in what was still out to be discovered than tracking and training others.

But this time she may have discovered too much as she and a group of Marines and a shape-shifter warrior are trapped back behind enemy lines and cut off from rescue. Now, against her better judgment, she must trust the man who came from the distant planet Veld and can do the impossible: change his body.

Sometimes action is better than words, especially under stress and enemy fire.

This book is a work of fiction. Names, characters, places, and incidents either are products of the author's imagination or are used fictitiously. Any resemblance to actual events or locales or persons, living or dead, is entirely coincidental.

Forgive the Beast
Copyright © 2023 M. Garnet
ISBN: 978-1-4874-3964-4
Cover art by SudaGraphics Inc

Published by eXtasy Books Inc

Look for us online at:
www.eXtasybooks.com

Forgive the Beast

By

M. Garnet

DEDICATION

To Ruthe and the Tuesday night Chat Group of TARA the local Tampa, FL chapter of RWA. Without their help I wouldn't have found the right title and the reason to finish this story.

NOTE

A special thanks to my two special nephews who not only served to protect our country (thank you for your service) but also went on to work at jobs that continued to help people. Their military experience has helped me with the right terms and correct attitudes of the marines in this story. I love these two men: Richard Bucklew and Robert Bucklew.

CHAPTER ONE

No thank you, Sir. I regret that I feel it will be necessary for me to refuse the offer to train on the privately owned satellites. I'm in the military to serve my country and my world.

Sergeant Margaret Bloom was trying to pay attention as she pushed her anger aside while she was being taken on a tour of the Micon Mining satellite. The words of her failed refusal were like a drumbeat in her brain that wouldn't stop.

She had spent the entire trip to this location cussing out her officers, her teachers, and the military. She added any other idiots who couldn't understand that she had a talent that should be used on Earth, not out in distant space helping money grabbing companies or aliens.

She was known by the nickname of Mags by her fellow workers and friends. The name might have been shortened from her first name, or perhaps it was because she often had magnifying lenses floating around her workplace.

Mags's talent was to look at small items that needed to be fixed and see precisely what she could fix. Some of this was her eyes that spotted wires or contacts misaligned. But she also had a feeling within herself when she needed to look deeper to find the problem.

A new mental device had been developed that would allow the military to fire weapons using their minds. Sergeant Bloom was leading a team that was installing these devices on some weapons. The problem was that it wouldn't work on all weapons, and not all personnel seemed to understand how to make it work.

Mags knew the problem was with the personnel. They

didn't believe it would work, and if they didn't believe, then their minds wouldn't connect with their weapon.

She had two major problems as she walked through the privately owned satellite. One was that she hated anything that took her away from the damp weather of Florida, and the other was that she didn't want the mind control rocker to belong to anything but rather to be her little baby. She could put it to military use. After all, she'd gone into the military for altruistic reasons. But she had real problems helping greedy private companies.

Walking through satellite, she had another problem. She had been sure that with her degrees and experience, she would always remain on Earth, serving the military in the Science Division. She had worked out of the old NASA facilities on the coast of Florida that had been turned into a military installation when the actual space flights had been moved to Texas and Michigan.

By now, Sergeant Margaret Bloom had worked inside this metal tin of a satellite for over a month and was starting to shed some of her anger. She could walk down to the end of the hall and through a large porthole see her home world.

Her refusal had fallen on deaf ears, but she still could work within this floating area above Earth.

"No thank you, Sir. I that it I feel will be necessary for me to refuse the offer to transfer to a distant satellite. I understand that there might be some problems out there with the mind control rocker, but I could fix anything better if I was back on Earth."

In the echo of the metal satellite, no one could hear the Commander and the company manager, but they heard the sergeant's voice.

Loud and clear was Mags's voice. "No, no, no. I don't do

off world, I don't do company stuff and I sure as hell don't work with alien shifters."

The guys in uniforms in the hallway all shifted uneasily. They knew the sergeant was on the way to being busted and possibly doing some dirty duty time.

Mags woke up as the deep spaceship was being unloaded.

For hours, she had provided explanations why she couldn't depart from Earth. Eventually she'd decided to speak to a field doctor. He'd given her a shot, and now she opened her eyes in an unfamiliar capsule shaped ship. Her mind told her she was in deep trouble.

A private looked in the bunkroom where she was trying to shake off the last of the shot.

"Oh good, you're awake. Ma'am, your gear is in the first locker and you need to dress for appearance at a briefing on the satellite in twenty minutes."

Mags waited until she got her tote from the locker and had her shoes on before she began kicking a blank wall and cussing. She knew where she was. She was on the end of a short ride on a deep spaceship called a Grabber.

With her background and intuition, she was probably one of the few people who rode this type of ship and knew about special magnetic engines that had been developed. They actually grabbed the thin magnetic lines that crossed the universe.

The engines and deep space were an accident discovered by astronomers who were studying the skies with small satellites strung out around Earth and sending information back to the offices of educated men interested in finding out if the stars talked to each other.

They had help when there was some talking going on out there. But it seemed danger sometimes came with some discoveries. There were others out there, and some were not friendly.

After the development of the grab engine, which made traveling to anywhere possible, it soon became evident that the military was as necessary as explorers. It was made aware that there were riches to be had. That meant that those big companies that were spending so much money fighting each other for resources on Earth to spend that same investment to go in a different direction.

As Bloom was getting her anger under control, she was thinking of one alien group they were fighting out in areas that companies wanted to settle and mine for rich ores. The Trios was a name that she had heard even in the labs. When she was working hooking up the weapons, she heard the soldiers talk about the three-man crews that the Trios always sent out and how their own commanders started sending out four-man crews.

Finally, Mags shut out the noise of these field marines, as she was more interested in getting a weapon ready they could use the next time their little minds let them go out to a foreign planet.

One of the minuscule pieces of metal used in the mind control rocker was Indium. This was a very rare metal that usually was the by-product of the production of other metals. Now it was said that there was a jungle planet called U231Z42 on the star charts that actually had Indium in a natural form on the planet.

With her anger in check and all that in mind, she grabbed her tote and dressed in a comfortable military uniform that was variegated blue, green, and purple. Her helmet was attached to the outside of the waterproof tote, as it was too bulky and needed to be nearby to be quickly slipped onto her head. She hated the helmet, as it made her feel enclosed and cut off from reality.

CHAPTER TWO

No thank you, Sir. I regret that I feel it will be necessary for me to refuse the offer to serve on this team. Mags felt the heat move to her face as anger surged again. *Control*, she whispered to herself. The man sitting with all the others standing around him was a colonel, and she knew he had the last word.

Unfortunately, when the Colonel looked up from the portable net in his hand, he had a deep frown. "Did that sound like an invitation, Sergeant?"

Now Mags stood up straight, assuming a good military posture. "Sir, perhaps it would help if I explained. I am an Intuitive Electronic and IT engineer. I am working on the new mind control rocker, attaching them to weapons and training marines to use the new item in the field. I'm not trained for field work, sir."

There, she thought, *that should sell me as a nerd.*

Mags heard the Colonel sigh, and everyone in the room stopped moving. That wasn't good.

"Sergeant Bloom, is it?" The Colonel looked down at his net, pulling up what she assumed was her bio. "When we put together an away team, we select the people very carefully. We need certain talents for specific jobs to work together in the field. The marine with the big sour look on his face at my left will be working with you and will lead your team.

Now, go to the cafeteria and get what will probably be your last hot meal. The rest of your team will meet in . . ." The Colonel looked over at the lieutenant.

A big tough marine with no markings on his standard field uniform frowned at her. "Briefing will be in thirty-six minutes precisely in the room next to the food room. That's all, sergeant."

Without a doubt, she'd been dismissed. With all the higher-ranked marines in the room, she held back her words and walked out into the hallway.

A guard pointed. "Mess is that way, sergeant."

She nodded and hung her military backpack tote over one shoulder. She had told the truth when she said she had no training for fieldwork, as the backpack was awkward. Oh, she had gone through all the physical training for a new inductee when she was contacted by the government and agreed to their offer. It was the day she graduated from MIT. They offered her a lab where she could help Professor Dunn work on the mind control issues.

She'd felt being in the marines was just window dressing. She had always played sports and kept herself healthy, so the basic training was a nice challenge.

Whenever the Master Sergeant got in her face, she just sucked it up, having the promise that in a short time she also would have that same emblem on her shirt. After basic training and with her instant upgrade, she still followed the workout training to keep her tall body in shape.

As a long legged woman of five foot ten inches, she could hold her own in the hand-to-hand combat training. She found it cleared her mind to return to her workbench and all the tiny wires and soldering.

Her intuitiveness soon had her working next to Dunn as they developed the rocker to become more sensitive. It was Bloom who pointed out the flaw, the reason the rocker didn't work all the time. Some marines just didn't believe in mind control.

She explained her theory to Professor Dunn, and they developed a test to choose which soldiers could use the rocker and weed out the ones who failed.

In the military, she had no trouble with weapons, as she was the one who constantly tore them apart and made them better. Under Dunn's instructions, she used her intuitive talents to look at other problems and broken items and see what needed to be changed or fixed. He also advised her to keep a lot of her talent hidden. She respected him and took his advice.

What she had forgotten about was that when you were in the service, you were in the service completely. You had to wear what they told you to wear, sleep where they told you to, and go where they wanted you. Here she was, in a company satellite far away from Earth, about to work with a team she hated.

She wondered if it could get any worse. She ate what was called a hot steak and egg sandwich and took the black gunk called coffee with a lot of sugar into the meeting room.

There she went to the back of the small room to look over the five others who were part of her team besides the lieutenant, and things just got worse.

A large figure that almost filled the doorway caused them to look up. "Good, our last man is here, so let's get this brief in order. Everyone find a seat."

Mags was glad as she looked at the big man who was dressed in what some would call native clothes. Mags knew he was a native from the planet below them with just the chart designation of U231Z42. Worse, in Mags's mind, this guy wasn't human, he was a shapeshifter.

Fighting to keep her stupid sandwich down and refusing the black gunk in front of her, she looked around, finding no way to escape. There was only the one door, and she would have to move past the hulk and the men.

Bloom was in the worst nightmare she had ever dreamed. She was away from Earth. She was on a greedy company satellite. She was being attached to an away team, and now there was an alien shape shifter that was going along as part of the team. She could not handle this — she was shaking already.

She heard nothing of what the lieutenant was saying at the front of the room as he pulled a big floating display. When enough of her eyes cleared, she saw the schematic of a strange spaceship floating in the air and slowly rotating. At last, she had something to take her mind off her stomach wanting to reject everything.

Ignoring the elephant in the room, she looked at the side shots that showed photos taken from a distance. This was not the shape of a ship built by workers of Earth. This was an alien spaceship. "It has not shown any life and has no damage," the lieutenant said.

Without thinking, Mags spoke. "There is damage." Suddenly, she squirmed — all eyes were focused on her where she sat in the back of the small room.

"Sergeant, we have had a ship on this location for five earth days. There are no blast holes."

So they didn't like interruptions. Still, Mags knew her intuition and what she had seen. "There are two seams that are much wider than they should be, like something erupted inside that ship."

Now the lieutenant was really frowning. "You have just looked at a couple of shots from the farthest distance in our room, and you think you know something about that ship that our own people didn't recognize?"

"Wait." This was the native. "Enlarge that second shot."

Mags shrank down in her seat, not sure she wanted the alien helping her.

"She's right. Look at that lower seam compared to the ones above it." The hulk looked back at her, but she would not meet his eyes. Damn, she hated being in this room, and her stomach was giving her problems again.

CHAPTER THREE

The away team was now in another smaller spaceship with a grab motor. The pilot was taking them in close to another small ship that held marines and scientists. These were the ones who had been watching this ship until a boarding team arrived.

This was when reality finally hit her. She wouldn't be able to put her lab coat on over her uniform and inhale the scent of hot solder in her workspace on Earth again. She was going to board an alien spacecraft accompanied by some war-trained marines and an alien shifter. She hated her life at this moment.

She was with the rest of the team, the only woman, as they were all hoo-rah front-line men, not to forget the male shifter who was more front line than she wanted to think about. She put as much distance as she could between herself and the beast from the jungle planet known only as U231Z42.

Bloom didn't know too much about that planet except Earth had fought several battles against the Trios to protect the natives. In basic training, she'd been shown studies of Trios, an alien race that was surprisingly like humans except they all had a very pale appearance.

It was theorized that their original home was from a planet that was more distant from their sun or from a sun with a slightly different spectrum. Regardless, when Earth doctors did a post-mortem examination of some of their soldiers, it was discovered they were comparable to humans. In fact, they were interchangeable if one wanted to breed. Mags cringed when that statement was put on the floating announcer. She hadn't realized she was bigoted in any manner until she learned more about aliens.

They had their own name in their own languages, but Earth had designated them Trios, as they used math in threes, traveled in threes, and built in threes. When her world's troops traveled, it was usually in two or more. The Trios went in three or more.

She knew her field troops now traveled in four or more to compensate for that reason. They wanted to be equal in the field against the enemy.

Mags was thinking of anything but what was happening to her as she sat next to Scanlon. The small narrow ship was set up with two men in front, the pilot and navigator. Behind them, without barriers, were two seats, each with the aisle down one side.

She had taken the seat next to the lieutenant, figuring she and were the only marines with some type of rank. The rest of the grunts sat behind them, with the hulk being the last guy to board. She heard his name called out as *Teve* when someone invited him to a seat.

"Damn shape shifter." Mags mumbled under her breath.

Evidently, she'd mumbled too loud, as Lt. Scanlon looked at her. "You know they are officially called modifiers. It is why the Wisoo people are interested in them. In their other form, they are almost indestructible. The Wisoo, or what we call Trios, hope they can use the science to make their own people stronger."

Mags looked over at Scanlon. "Why doesn't he wear a uniform?"

Scanlon smiled in a wicked marine way. "If you ever see him change, you will understand his clothes. By the way, that was a good catch on the crack on the seam."

Bloom nodded and adjusted her backpack, pushing it

under her feet. She pulled her weapon into her lap, as she hadn't hooked it to her chest sling.

"Hey, is that one of the new MA Twelve with the rocker mind control? I thought they still had problems with that gadget." Scanlon reached for her weapon.

She let him have it, as there was no way he could trigger it or damage it in any way.

"Tell me how it works again?" Scanlon asked as he turned the field weapon over.

"There is a small device put behind the ear that connects a soldier who qualifies. I actually have an implant." Mags tapped her head behind her ear.

"So, if something happens to you, no one else can shoot this gun?"

Mags frowned and took back the gun. "Except for this small attachment right here . . ." She pointed at a piece that looked like part of the gun on its side . . . "Anyone can shoot the gun in the ordinary way. I can shoot it without pulling the trigger. Even while it is in your hands."

They both heard the click of the cylinder and they almost dropped down as he looked at the weapon without her hands anywhere near the trigger guard.

"Don't worry, per usual travel orders, it isn't loaded." Mags smiled as she tapped the long barrel. "You can't imagine the hours Professor Dunn and I worked to get the control rocker working. We threw out so many samples before we found out the problem wasn't with our product. It was, oh, I'm sorry, I always get carried away when talking about lab work."

She looked through the front view, past the shoulders of the pilot. "Lieutenant, I don't belong out here. I am a lab rat. I make things for guys like you. I hate space and am afraid of these grabber ships. Worst of all, I have a deep dislike of anything alien, starting with the big guy in the back seat and counting in the Trios and whatever made that thingy out there."

The lieutenant made a huffing noise. "Sorry, Sarge, but they picked every one of us for a reason. Well except me, I am just here to keep you guys on the right path and alive."

To keep her mind off what was going to happen next, she asked for details. "So, tell me what the other five guys are expert in."

Scanlon rolled his eyes. "Okay, maybe it will help you fit in with this group. I have worked with them before. Deeks is an expert in rare metals. Thomlinson is a rock climber and electrons guy. Tumbler is a sharpshooter, but he can't shoot a mind control rocker. He carries a weapon he built himself.

Aero is our Trio expert, spent the last two years in their backyard with Teve. Simkowski is our contact expert. He can beat a stick on a rock and get a message all the way to Earth."

They were thinking for a moment. "As for Teve, he is our protection. There are some things out here away from Earth that are just better than what we are or what we have."

"I have to ask, why am I on this team?"

Scanlon looked over at the tall woman holding the weapon he had heard so many negative words about and saw a pretty face with short blond hair and very light blue eyes. She wasn't the most beautiful woman in magazine covers, but he would buy her a beer in the local bar. Right now, in the marines, she was strictly hands off for a Lieutenant.

"Sergeant, I don't know. I just follow orders. They told me to take Teve and an Earth lab rat. They sent me you."

Mags shifted in the seat as she looked around the small capsule shaped ship. There was no need for sleek, pointed vehicles in space, as there was no friction to battle. Mags thought they could just shoot boxes through space with a grab engine.

With that, her mind was busy thinking of all the shipping containers gathering rust in all the old seaports of the world.

She pulled out her net comm that was the size of an old-fashioned credit card. She expanded it to the size of her hand and made some notes on boxes and containers.

The pilot spoke quietly over the floating comm in the center of the small ship they were riding. "You want us to swing around it or approach or anything special? Are you guys looking for a door or hatch?"

Scanlon nodded. "Pull in close and rotate around it."

"Go to the ends." Mags was sorry as soon as she spoke, feeling eyes on her from the back as well as Scanlon's.

"Why?" Scanlon's question was terse.

She ducked her head and shrugged. "How do we get into our capsule?"

Everyone, including the pilot, looked at the hatch at the back of their small ship.

Scanlon looked at the pilot. "Try the ends. Stay about nine meters out at first."

They hit paydirt on the first pass. The whole end looked like it had two entrances. One was a large, obviously covered lock that would open large enough to let a ship larger than the one they were in enter easily. On one side of that larger door was a smaller lock that was for smaller items to enter or exit. Now all they had to do was figure out how to get it opened. Up close, this ship, if it was a ship, was mammoth.

Scanlon stood up. "Okay, I need to send a couple over to see if we can get that small door open."

Tumbler spoke first. "Boss, besides shooting, I know how to blow things up. Maybe a little explosive would work."

"No." Mags actually yelled and then stepped back. "Sorry." She hated it when everyone looked at her.

"The sarge is right." Scanlon said. "We need to try an easy way first. Ski, suit up and take the sergeant with you. Take a look. With your electronics knowhow and her intuition, maybe you can find a door handle."

"Uh, I have never been in a suit in space." Mags looked around, and she was sure her face reflected her panic.

Simkowski, whose nickname was Ski, was already up and, with help, was pulling out the off-ship suits.

He winked at his buddies. "Don't worry Sarge, I'll help you. I always wanted to tell a sergeant what to do."

The suits that were now called off-ship suits had once also been called space suits. The original fledgling astronauts in their big white bulky suits with the large air containers would not recognize the suits that were now used to protect humans from the void of space.

Both Mags and Ski stripped off their boots and uniforms, down to the standard long blue underwear they both wore. It was comprised of a pair of pants that reached to the ankles and a top that hugged the body to the wrists.

In training, she had often stripped to such an outfit in front of a man, but in these tight quarters, she turned her back and tried to ignore any looks. Putting on the off-ship suit was like pulling on a rubber under-water suit. It was made of some type of gel that covered the body from toes to finger and up to the neck.

A ring that would connect to the helmet was then fitted around the neck. The helmet was clear on three sides, but up the back and over the top was a lot of extra equipment. It was manipulated via from buttons on top or from contacts on the wristband each of them was donning. There also was a stand-ard belt that contained some tools and a weapon.

They added a backpack that attached flat and low to the butt area which contained a full field outfit they could change into later.

Mags refused the weapon and pointed to her long gun. She reversed the chest strap and let her gun hang down her back between the two containers. These held what would convert to air and could also push her through the void.

The idea this time was just to go out and push off their ship to glide over to the big item blocking their view. There seemed to be a lot of knobs, bolts and odd items that they could grasp once they were next to the strange alien ship. From this close up, the floating vessel seemed to be more of a long rectangle than a capsule like all the spaceships humans had constructed. It had points at each end, but they didn't have a clue which one might be the front and which was the rear.

Ski talked to Mags through their helmet comm, but it was also being broadcast inside their ship. "Here's the scoop, Sarge. We will hook together. Don't do anything but relax until we hit that ship. Then grab something, anything. I will work the push to get us over there. Okay?"

He was snapping a short line to her waist belt as he was talking, not really expecting her to answer or agree. He was the expert in space walking, and he clearly expected her to just follow.

As for Mags, she wished she had found the time to use the john before getting into the suit, as she was afraid she was going to piss in her long underwear. She also was determined not to let any of these men see her fear. She took a deep breath and responded. "Lead on, soldier." She even stepped to the airlock first.

The length of their tether was about ten feet, so they both held some of it rolled up to keep it off the floor. She immediately felt the difference as their suits hugged them when the air left the lock.

Ski punched the flat numbers on the keypad to allow the exterior door to open. He reached out to hold onto a long rail on the outside and she slowly floated out, still keeping close to him by holding some of the tether.

When she was clear, the hatch closed, and he nodded at

her. "Okay, let go of the tie as I am going to push off. We will both be jerked, but don't let that worry you. As long as you don't do anything, it will slow us down a little, but we will still go toward the alien ship. Like I said before. When we get there, grab anything."

The trip was exactly as Ski described. The tether pulled and floated and pulled, and she was frightened more than she had ever been in her life. She just knew that she was not meant to be out here in nothing. All she could do was keep her eyes on the dancing tether and know she was about to die.

CHAPTER FOUR

Suddenly, Mags realized the tether was bunching up. She looked up and saw she was about to slam into a large black piece of metal with a couple of knobs sticking right out at her. Reaction caused her to reach out and grab a handle to keep from being poked in the face. She was alive.

"Hey, Ski, I have a handhold."

"Me too, Sarge." Ski's voice was clear in her helmet. "I'm right below you."

She heard some grunting, and then Ski spoke again. "I'm unhooking us, so be sure you hang onto something or turn on some magnetics."

Mags knew that both the bottom of her suit shoes and her flat hands were magnetic if she turned them on. She left the tether still hooked to her and tilted her body to look down to see where Ski was trying to move on the flat surface with all its knobs. He was headed to her right.

"Ski, you're going the wrong way."

There was a grunt. "You sure? I can't tell anything when we're this close."

Another voice spoke. "The intuitive female is correct."

It was the voice of the shifter, and Mags almost cussed out loud. She sucked in a deep breath. There might be some advantage to being out here, away from anyone in the small ship.

Ski began moving in the other direction, and she could see several items that she could grip that would let her get down to his level. Being very careful and not looking behind her at the great expanse of space, she made her way down to where Ski was stationed in front of what had looked like an entrance hatch.

If the entities that built this object were in any way similar to humans, then this hatch would allow the entrance of anyone from their small ship, including the native.

"Okay, what do we see? I don't see the loo's door handle. I also don't see any type of pad or something that might be electronic that we touch, rub, kiss or hit that might open this door. What does your magic tell you?"

Moving in front of the hatch as Ski scooted over to allow her to examine the possible opening, she tried to think how she would design a system to allow her to get back in if no one was home. She would make it easy, because she might be hurt or she could be bringing in a hurt comrade.

That would mean that she would only have one hand free and she couldn't hang on to anything. *Think, Mags, think like you do when you are in your lab.* Now she was talking to herself as she looked at the large door and finally saw the secret.

There were three or four holes in the middle of the door. One was a few inches from the top, with one at about her shoulder height. Another one was close to her stomach, and the fourth was below her feet.

Before she moved, she decided to take precautions. "Ski, take hold of the tether again. I might get blown in or away when I open this door."

She waited until she felt the pull on the tether, then she carefully placed herself in front of the door. She held onto a knob at the side, and in no gravity, she lowered her body until her feet were in front of the bottom hole. Her body covered the middle hole, so she raised her arm, twisting her body just a little so her arm and hand covered the two top holes.

Instantly, the door disappeared. She was first blown outward, then sucked into a dark maw. The tether pulled tight, but gravity also pulled her down to a floor. She let out an *oomph.*

"Sarge, you okay?"

She used her wrist control and light. "I'm okay. Come on in."

Ski worked his way around the opening, then stepped into the gravity. Unfortunately, as soon as he cleared the entrance, the door appeared again, and it was closed.

"Hey, Lieutenant, can you guys hear us?" Ski tried to reach the small ship.

"Loud and clear." Scanlon's voice was all business. "Don't go any further. We will be over. How did you open the door, Sergeant?"

Mags tried to keep her voice calm. "There are four small holes about the size of a dime up and down the middle of the door. Float in front and let your single body cover all four holes at once. The door will disappear. Enter fast."

Both Ski and Mags looked around in the dark as far as their helmet lights would penetrate. Mags returned to the door to inspect the surrounding plates. There were several that were dark at about shoulder height. The walls were made of black metal and didn't have any bolts, yet they had seams.

She put her gloved finger on a narrow seam that ran even with the floor and just started walking. She had probably gone fifty feet before Ski yelled.

"Sarge, where ya' goin'?"

Mags smiled to herself as she turned her helmet to shine on the other wall, something she had done every four or five steps. "Just following the breadcrumbs, soldier boy."

At that moment, she turned at the noise as the rest of the team came through the door. They not only added light in the entrance, but they had a couple of large hand-held lights.

Now, her breadcrumbs had led her to home, or at least she could see an end. She saw another wall and searched it with her helmet light. It looked like it could go up into the ceiling, yet there was a door about the size of the one they had come in from outside. This door was on one side of the end wall. She would know more as she got closer.

There was mumbling and movement from behind her, and she heard a man say something about getting back out of the door. She also heard them talking to their pilot, who could still hear them.

The team moved up to where she was standing and the stronger lights showed a better view of the outline of the inside door.

"What do you think, Deeks?" Scanlon asked the metal expert. The smaller man walked up to the door and looked around.

"Don't know, Loo. I don't see any holes this time."

"She knows."

Mags heard the voice of the alien and almost fell to the floor. She fought to get air, thinking her suit respiration had failed. He was there, right behind her. There was no place for her to go, and without air, she would pass out before she died from suffocation.

It took her only seconds to know that she was suffering from a full-blown panic attack. Her heart was racing, her lungs were not processing the air molecules, and her legs were refusing to hold her up.

Scanlon moved up beside her, and just the presence of a human male let something in her relax. She turned slowly, her light crossing over the faces of the men. Teve had stepped back away from her. Had he felt her fear? It didn't matter, as long as he stayed away.

"Okay Sarge. Is Teve correct? What do you see? Are we trapped in a storage area?"

She stooped over and put her hands on her knees and waited for her body to get steady. At last, she could speak.

"We are in an airlock."

Aero came up and moved around the sergeant. He rubbed his hand on a plate on the door. "She's right. Not only that, but it looks like there is an atmosphere of some type inside this ship."

What he was doing was rubbing frost off a window.

"Okay, but there are no holes to open this door. Sarge, how do we get inside?"

Chapter Five

A fter Mags put her hand over one hole, there was a lot of noise, a deep rumble, and actually some shaking. When the atmosphere came in, it was white smoke at first as it hit the cold, and then it began to spread out. Eventually, the fog cleared out, and she felt her suit loosen. The atmosphere must be close to Earth's atmospheric pressure at sea level.

There was a click, and the entrance door opened. There were also some lights that came on the other side of the wall. The lights were somewhat soft and blue.

Aero spoke. "Oh, oh. Wisoosio. Trio colors. Everyone, take care. Teve, come up here, and we will go in first." He didn't have to ask them .

Mags had her body working again and moved back to let everyone else enter the ship. Again, once they were all past the entrance door, it closed.

Scanlon tried their ship again. "Contact Bird, can you hear us?"

"Loud and clear."

"Okay, we seem to be inside the ship, and there is some kind of atmosphere. We will run tests."

Scanlon looked over at his team. "Deeks, tell me what type of atmosphere is surrounding us on this ship?"

"It's not a ship," mumbled Mags.

"It's not the Wisoo," stated Teve.

Now everyone but Deeks turned around to look at the two team members who were talking so softly. Both Mags and Teve were standing far apart, and both were flashing their

22

helmets up and around at the seams in the walls where they all stood.

"Wait." Thomlinson looked at the sergeant, who was looking up. He also looked up and saw only a metal ceiling. "What do you see, Sarge, that I don't see?"

She brought her head down and kept her light out of Thomlinson's eyes. "How many people could you house in this containment unit?"

Thomlinson looked at her, puzzled. "I don't know. I could guess maybe, oh, five thousand."

Scanlon cleared his throat. "It could contain up to ten thousand, depending on what we can make out. But on the other hand, there might be only a couple hundred people, if the rest of the area is for storage and moving items from place to place."

Tumbler grunted. "A giant storage shed. Maybe it just drifted away and someone is looking for it."

Scanlon waved a hand for silence. "Deeks, what kind of atmosphere is in here?"

Deeks tapped his small equipment. "It looks good, heavy on the oxygen and small traces of carbon monoxide."

Scanlon stepped to Deeks. "What does that mean?"

Deeks smiled. "We will feel good because of lots of oxygen and the carbon monoxide is not any more than what Aero farts in his sleep."

There were a couple of chuckles. Deeks reached up and removed his helmet. Every one of the team just froze and watched Deeks, probably to see if he fell down in spasms on the floor as the poison air hit his lungs. Instead, he just took a deep breath and did a thumbs-up motion. Mags would soon learn that when in the field, there were no tricks for jokes among these marines.

Just to add to the interest, the inner door opened.

Tumbler and Teve went through the door first, Tumbler

with his special weapon out as he crouched in that marine way of approaching danger. Teve moved a few feet away and also hunched over, his eyesight better in the blue light of the long hallway. Both men took a few steps, then Tumbler threw a cleaning net. It was just a mixture of soft rubber like threads and smoke that spread out ahead of the men to trigger any traps.

There were no arrows from the walls and no big ball rolling down the hall, so the fog cleared and the thin strips just settled in pretty colors on the floor. That meant the floor was also safe.

Scanlon started for the door as he gave orders. "Okay, everyone inside. Take turns taking off your big backpack and changing into your field uniforms. We will leave the off-ship suits here. Ski, attach a locater to our stuff, so we can find it when we need it. Keep Sarge in the middle, and we will start down into the ship."

"If it's a ship," mumbled Mags.

"Okay." Scanlon glanced over at the young woman. "We will keep an open mind."

Everyone was now in their blue multi color uniforms, boots and weapons. That was, all but Teve. Mags kept looking at him out of the corner of her eye, shocked at what he was wearing. He was a large muscular man dressed in a sleeveless shirt and pants that laced up the outside of each leg, showing the tan skin of his body. This was completed with long soft boots that allowed him to move with no sound.

They all had an earbud that fed them contact with each other and the small outside ship except for Mags. Her implants could be coded to act as receivers.

Their larger wristbands allowed them to turn on thermal imaging in limited degrees, some radar and some sound emitters. The wrist controls could also give them heat or cooling within their uniforms. It would also send a silent signal if the wearer was incapacitated.

They walked in this formation for about thirty minutes when Aero made a mention of the walls. "Good lighting, but no doors."

Without thinking, Mags spoke. "We have passed several doors, they just blend in with the seams."

Scanlon turned and faced her. "You know Sarge, I understand you have been locked up in some lab by yourself, but you have to share with us when you see something. That is why the Colonel stuck us with you."

"Okay." Mags answered in a surly manner. "Up ahead, the hallway ends and it splits in two ways."

Tumbler and Teve jogged ahead for another twenty minutes, almost to that point, and were carefully checking out both directions. "Which way, Loo?" asked Tumbler.

"Neither," snarled Mags.

Evidently tired of Mags's un-marine-like actions, Scanlon reached down and held her by an upper arm. Then they walked fast to stand between Tumbler and Teve.

"Which way?"

"Leave go of me. Open your eyes. The clear box straight ahead is an elevator."

Tumbler was shooting the cleaning nets down both side hallways. Teve turned to the side. "She is right. Ship or storage unit, the command center would be at the top."

Areo spoke as he walked up. "Can we operate that thing?"

"Can we trust it?" This came from Deeks.

Mags decided it was time to say more than just grumble. "You guys remember how big this thing is. Even if we find some stairs, how long is it going to take us to climb to the top?"

Tumbler went over and put his hand over a hole. There was a sound like air moving, but they felt nothing. They were all careful to face back-to-back in all directions. Mags and

Teve were the ones who watched the clear box. They saw its floor move down and then stop as the front doors opened.

At the noise of the doors opening, the rest of the marines glanced at the elevator.

"Well, that answers how we get it to respond to us." Aero looked around but was still on full alert.

"A conundrum. I hate to put all the team in a small alien box, but I also hate to break us up."

"Hey, Loo, I vote we all die together." This came from Deeks, holding up some type of explosive.

Scanlon nodded. "Keep that out in case this is a trap. Everyone, into the glass box and weapons ready."

It got silent in the box as Mags was jammed against the wall between Tumbler and Aero. Deeks was pushing against her side with his weird explosive in one hand and his automatic energy weapon in the other. Like her weapon, his weapon was also attached to his chest by a belt that helped keep it in place.

"Okay Sarge, how do we tell it to take us up to the top?" This was from Aero, who was in front of her.

She looked around him and saw all the holes. "I think you take your hand below all the holes and just raise it up over all of them until you clear the top."

"That's a lot of guess-work." Someone grumbled, but Aero did what she suggested and they moved up.

Ski tried their small ship but got no answer. "Anyone get an answer from the ship?"

There were some clicks and soft mumbles, but no good response.

There was a nod. "Everyone, check their contact with the team."

There was the click and buzz as the response came from each member in their ears, including Mags. Member contact was good. Everyone watched the floors moving past as they went up. At one time there were some figures, not moving, at the door.

"What the fuck was that?" Thomlinson yelled. He had his nose to the clear door, but they were moving too fast and they were past it before anyone could say anything.

Now everyone was staring out through the clear front doors. There were some changes, as some areas were dark without lights. Some hallways had lights that were brighter, like the lights they had attached to their belts.

They didn't see anything resembling figures again. The elevator stopped, but the doors didn't open. The area in front of them wasn't a hallway, but a large, endless room. From their angle, they couldn't see the end and it seemed to be empty.

"Should we try to open the door?" This was from Aero.

"It doesn't look like a command center." Scanlon leaned over Thomlinson.

"Well, we can't just stand here in a glass can." This was from Deeks with his explosives.

"It's not the top yet." Mags just had a feeling about this place. "It might have been programmed to stop here by the last guy that used it. Aero, wave your hand from bottom to top again."

Aero repeated the wave, and they started moving. She felt eyes on her she ignored as the floors flashed past. The next time they stopped, the doors opened.

Everyone in the elevator froze, and not even Mags had a smart remark.

CHAPTER SIX

The final floor that the elevator stopped on looked exactly like a storage area. But the question was, what was it storing? There were rows and rows of hundreds of hanging body shaped containers.

Aero and Thomlinson, being in front, moved out slowly and stepped to each side of the elevator to take up sentry positions. Mags pressed against the wall of the elevator to let the others slowly ease out into the room.

Scanlon looked over his shoulder at her. "Think you can figure out how to get the elevator to go down a floor, Sarge?"

Mags was glad to have a job that she understood, even if she couldn't figure it out. She stooped over in front of the palm box with the holes. There were no lights within any of the holes.

She nodded. "So they are simply sensor devices. Probably respond to the warmth in our hands."

Deeks was still beside her, with Teve beside him. Teve was watching the men outside the doors and Deeks reached a finger over a hole.

"You mean . . . shit" The door closed immediately, and they moved down fast.

Deeks jumped back, still clutching his explosive in one hand, pulling his weapon forward with the other. Teve was in a muscular crouch. Mags, against the wall, felt her weapon move up into her hands in response to her thought.

They had all taken this reflex because the elevator stopped and the doors opened. The area in front of them was black, without lights. There was silence, as all three were holding their breaths, waiting.

When nothing happened after a couple of seconds, Deeks shifted position first. He spoke in a whisper. "Sorry, that was stupid. Sarge, cover the top button and let's join the team."

His next effort was to reach the team through his earbud. There was no response. "Sarge, try your contact."

She moved her hand to cover the top button, and nothing happened. "Deeks, maybe it takes your long reach to be able to hit the button in the correct manner."

Deeks put away the explosive and reached over to cover the top button, but nothing happened. He opened his hand and waved it from bottom to top. Nothing happened. He waved down, covered different buttons, trying both hands, letting the sling hold his weapon, and still nothing happened.

Deeks held up his hands. "Sarge, any more suggestions?"

Suddenly, Teve stepped out through the doors. His voice was gravelly and low so that it wouldn't carry far. "We'll find the stairs she mentioned before and go up to join the team."

Mags took a moment to try to contact the team. "Sorry, Deeks, I can't hear anything either. Something is blocking us, maybe the floors."

Deeks stepped from the elevator, pulled out one of the larger lights, and flashed it around. The darkness ate it up—there was nothing close that reflected his light.

Teve kept his voice low. "I see nothing. It seems to be empty."

Coming out slowly, her weapon in her hand, Mags kept Deeks between her and the beast. *You're not in Kansas anymore, Dorothy.* She was so far from her controlled and neat lab.

"Which way, Sarge? Any guesses?" Deeks was still flashing his light back and forth.

Mags attached a sharp penlight to her shoulder that would turn with her and light the floor ahead of her without spreading. "The entrance we used seemed to be more toward one end of the construction than on the other. We need to go to one of the sides, since we can't get to the front with this wall in our way."

Deeks hesitated. "You think they had stairs on both sides of their ship?"

Teve spoke in a whisper. "That is the way I would build it."

"Wait." Mags took a moment to think and catch up on her intuitions. With her back to the elevator, that meant the place they'd entered was in front of her, down a long distance of blackness.

So if this was a ship and there was a front and back, then the front was behind the elevator and wall. Even in a ship, but especially if they were inside some type of container, there would be steps at the sides. *Therefore, follow the wall.*

Keeping her light at a point where it also reflected on the wall, she started walking. She tried to keep her steps toe to heel so that her steps were quiet. Still, she heard Deeks's heavy boots behind her. She didn't hear the shifter, but she hoped he was still third in line, with a fair distance between them. This was going to be a long walk.

Aero was on his knees in front of the palm plate of the elevator while Tumbler covered his back. Scanlon and Ski were carefully looking over the hanging body-shaped items.

Scanlon decided they would examine the first one to see if they could see inside or get it open without making noise or a fuss. First, they used some of the fog shots. They didn't want to have the strings from the other type of clearing nets clutter the hanging shapes.

They were sacrificing their own weapons by scooting them on the floor to clear a safe area that they could walk across.

They laid their weapons side by side on the floor and Aero stood on the back end of both, hopefully putting enough weight on the entire length to avoid triggering any explosion or gas dispersal.

He then used his legs to slide them slowly apart about two feet, with Scanlon holding him from behind. They repeated the steps over and over until they were up against the first hanging shape.

Now they carefully slid the weapons further apart, each stepping on an end, giving them a wider area to examine the item in front of them.

"Well, Loo, what next?"

Scanlon kneeled down on one heel and looked up at the large dark frame. "I wish we had the sarge and her intuition with us."

"Yep, or Deeks's magic hand." With that, Aero reached up and swiped his hand down the front of the hanging figure. Both he and Aero jumped back as the black cloth folded away and dropped to the floor.

What was left hanging by its shoulder pads was a heavy suit of armor with an empty helmet and attached boots and gloves. It was all in matte black and looked like metal. It was large, but still Scanlon thought it might fit him with some adjustments.

"Protective armor." Aero whispered those words.

"Battle armor," Scanlon said, correcting his soldier.

By this time, Tumbler had joined them. "How many do you think are in here?"

Scanlon took a long stride sideways to look down in the distance between the rows. The rows disappeared in the long room until it was impossible to count. "Hard to say, as many as several thousand or more."

Thomlinson approached and scooted up onto another hanging battle suit. From this position, he could see a distance into the room. "I would estimate about ten thousand sets of armor, if they are all full of the same thing."

Ski whistled behind them. "An army. That would outfit a big army."

"Yeah, but where are they right now?" Aero looked around as he spoke.

"How many floors did we pass coming up here?" Ski was returning to the elevator as he spoke out loud. "Even worse, did we get on the elevator on the first floor or in the middle? Were there floors below where we entered?"

"First, we need to get our team back together. The sarge mentioned something about climbing stairs. Anyone have an idea where we might find some way to go down besides that fucking useless elevator?" Scanlon growled as he returned to the wall by the elevator.

Aero was looking both ways down the wall that was against the elevator. "Hey, guys, is this wall the back or the front of the ship? I mean the other side, or is it just halfway through? There could be a whole section on the other side of this wall." He walked along, tapping on the wall. It rang the same as he moved.

Scanlon nodded. "Okay men, let's follow Aero. Eventually, it should lead us to a door or a corner. Stay alert."

Aero looked over his shoulder. "Loo, that armor was not made to fit a Trio."

No one made a response to that observation. Aero was their expert on the Wisoo people that most called the Trio. Aero had spent two years with the natives on the jungle planet that both Earth and the Wisoo had first wanted to claim.

It turned out that the two peoples wanted it for different reasons. Mining corporations had first found the planet was rich in rare minerals, especially Indium. Normally on Earth, Indium was a by-product in the smelting and combining of other metals.

The planet known on the star charts as U231Z42 seemed to have this rare metal and several more. When rich mining corporations from Earth moved in, they ran into two problems — the were natives on the planet, and another off-world group that was also interested in it. Humans had fought several skirmishes with the Trios, but this site had become the first real war.

It seemed the Trios were more interested in the natives than in the metals on the planet. Earth had a whole system set up to protect planets with natives. These natives were unusual. They were especially intelligent and had progressed in some ways beyond Earth science in natural physical and life sciences.

The natives were called modifiers, because they could change their entire bodies into a stronger, faster, better and larger entity that made them impervious to most weapons and dangerous if they were provoked.

Although Earth wanted metals and minerals from the unusual planet, the Wisoo people wanted the secret behind the natives in order to make their own armies stronger. The war was still going on within that planet, although it was now covert.

Earth would respond to a notice of a Trio compound and send in troops. Aero had spent two years on the ground with the natives in order to find the buried compounds of the Trios. The problem was that when they found them, the Trios had left no traces of life.

Teve had told Aero once, around a campfire, that the Trios would never succeed transferring the modifier gene to their people. He explained part of the process was in believing. Teve said that Trios never would believe that it could be done by mental thought, just that they would find an outside trigger to make it work. Teve shrugged and explained it would never work with a trigger.

The amazing discovery made by Earth anthropologists was that not all the natives were modifiers. It seemed somewhere in evolution on this planet, a group of special warriors had emerged to meet their needs.

CHAPTER SEVEN

It seemed to Sergeant Margret Bloom that they had walked forever in this black metal room, following the single metal wall.

"Freeze." This was a whispered word from Teve.

Both Mags and Deeks didn't question the murmured word. For Deeks, he was used to working as a team and listening to whatever help a teammate might offer. For Mags, it was just distaste of the beast and fear of their position in the dark. She also didn't move her shoulder, leaving that the light held in one position, on the floor and wall in front of her.

At this point they all heard two noises. There was a thump on the wall next to them that made Mags jump away. The second noise was out in the darkness, and it was a shuffling sound.

"Fuck." Deeks sighed as he moved his weapon up and toward the unlit room. "Teve, don't change until we identify the threat."

"True." The sound of his voice was from a different direction, and Mags jerked again as she realized he had moved in the inky blackness of the area.

There was a thump on the wall again.

Deeks moved over to Mags so he could whisper. "Do you think this wall is the end, the outside, or the middle of this ship?"

Mags reached up and turned her light to dim. Now that Deeks was speaking to her, she was calming down. Her flight=or=fight reflexes were under control, and her scientific attentiveness was in the front of her brain.

As quietly as possible, she spoke to Deeks. "I know we walked deep, but I don't think we made it all the way through to the other side." She looked again, as there was another thump back at the area where she had been standing. Had something sensed that something warm blooded was standing close to the wall back there? Mags took another step away from the wall.

When she heard the shuffling noise that was maybe coming closer, she noticed a blue light flickering off and on,

Deeks spoke a little louder. "Teve, are you out in front of us? Should we turn on more light to help you?"

"No need, I can see fine. We are about to be visited by a small machine. At this point, we can't trust it."

Deeks was down on a knee with his weapon against his cheek. With her weapon responding to her mind, she stood to one side of Deeks, not even needing to point the MA12. It would shoot where she wanted it to and at what she desired, with just a thought.

The shuffling got louder and finally Deeks unhooked and turned on his big flash. A square garbage can on treads was rolling towards them. They all stepped back to give it room as it continued to roll up to the wall where the thump had come from and then stopped. It squeaked once, settled down on the floor and its blue light shut off.

Deeks carefully walked up to the small square can that had quit moving and nudged it with the end of his gun. Mags noted it was waist high to Deeks and about two feed square. There were a lot of holes and what looked like small doors on the side she could see.

Deeks nudged it again. "Okay R2D2, can you do anything else but respond to a wall thump?"

Teve's voice came from the darkness. "There are doors on the side of him or it."

Deeks was about to put his weapon in back of his shoulder. but Mags interrupted him. "Hold up, Deeks, you are a bit too quick on the draw. Let me."

Mags took Deeks's place and kneeled at the plain side of the moving box that was still bumping the wall. Her mind told her that the plain side was the safe side. Any protection would be by the doors that were on each side.

She made sure her hands were free and then she looked behind her. "You guys stay back."

She heard Deeks's shuffle, but sighed when she knew Teve moved, yet she heard nothing from his large body. One handle was further away, and the other was close to her. Her hope was that they would open easily and not require all her strength just to give an uneven pull.

Taking a breath and then holding it, she reached in, grabbed both handles, and yanked. One door opened against the wall and the other came toward her. With this action, the box quit moving against the wall. To her relief, there were no explosives shooting out of either side.

She felt the safest way to see inside was to stand and lean over the top to look in one side and then into the other. She finally reached in and came out with what might look like a strange gun.

Deeks moved further back and spread his light to a bigger glow. "Is that a weapon?"

Mags brought out some silver cloth from the other side. She turned and leaned against what Deeks had nicknamed R2D2. "Well, in some ways, it is a gun. This little unit is some type of triage unit. My guess is this gun shoots meds, and this wad is probably wrapping for wounds. There are tubes that are probably some types of meds. It responded to whatever thumped on the wall."

Deeks stepped closer. "So, something alive is hurt beyond the wall and needs help."

Teve had moved over into the very edge of the light with his hand on the wall. "I don't think there is anything alive beyond the wall at this point."

Deeks brought his weapon back up. "So, something was alive and ran off or just died behind that wall."

"Or something inanimate thumped the wall." Mags spoke as she looked closer at the items in the box. "There might be a triage unit on the other side that ran out of little blue pills and called for a friend."

Deeks tried to contact the team again and got silence. "I got nothing from the ship or the team."

Mags got up with a couple of vials. "Well, we might as well continue our trek to the stairs. I'm going to take some samples that we could research when we get back to our ship."

"Hey, Sarge, what if we are going up one set of stairs and the rest of the team is coming down another one?"

"Damn, we need to go back to the elevator and leave a note." Mags frowned as she searched and poked, coming out with a marker.

Teve moved up. "I can travel faster than both of you. Tell me what to write." He held out a thickset hand for the marker.

Mags moved away from him and into Deeks's wide light. She turned to the wall above the triage box. On the wall, she drew an arrow in the direction they were heading. Above it, she drew a few connected steps going up and then a question mark.

"How about that, Deeks? Think that will give our guys a message if they make it this far?"

Deeks nodded approval, and Teve took the marker and moved off without a sound into the darkness.

Deeks grunted. "The more I'm around that guy, the more I understand why the Trios want some of his DNA."

"He's more animal than human." Mags's low worded statement sounded like a curse.

Deeks moved his light to look at her. "Hey, Sarge, I thought you lab rats had open minds. That sounded a bit prejudiced."

Without an answer, she turned and started on down the wall, again using her own penlight. As she walked, she could still hear Deeks moving around the square triage unit. Next, she heard him jogging to catch up with her, so she just stopped.

Deeks's wide light hit her and she turned to shield her eyes. Looking down, she saw the soft boots of the beast in the edge of the circle, so he had made a quick return. She turned and led the way into the darkness.

They had walked for almost another hour when Deeks spoke up. "Sarge, I think it's time for a break. I have a bladder that is squeezing me and I could use some protein."

Her reaction was disgust. They would eat field rations that were not too bad, but they had to use field latrine bags and take all their trash with them. She looked around and noted that at least they had lots of privacy with all the darkness.

It took them a while to get the uncomfortable part done and then to eat. Mags drew their sign on the wall again and smiled as she added a crude drawing of an old-fashioned toilet. She also added the time.

Deeks was trying to contact everyone and anyone but could only talk by earbud to Mags and Teve.

CHAPTER EIGHT

Deeks turned to Mags with his bright light, pointing down, picking up the soft boots of Teve. She hadn't known the native was that close. Of course not, as stealth was part of the beast's M.O. She fought not to show any reaction.

Deeks was speaking. "Sarge, I want to see if it is the floors that are interfering with our contact. I want to get ahead. You will be able to see me with this bright light, but I will jog while you two just walk. Let's see if some distance between us in this room makes hearing each other a problem."

Without any more discussion, he was off with his light on bright and broadest circle. Mags kept walking, watching it move up and down with his movements.

It took a while for a range to build up between them, but eventually, the light began to shrink. She was shocked to hear the shifter speak.

"I am about ten feet behind you and in the dark. I know I make you uncomfortable, but I don't want to get too far away."

Mags couldn't help but snort. *Sure, a beast with feelings.* She wouldn't bite on that one. She looked behind her, letting her fingers trail on the wall and didn't see even a shadow of the seven-foot tall native behind her. *How could someone that big move that silently?*

She looked forward at the pinpoint of Deeks's light. She reached up and touched her implant. "Hey, Deeks, can you hear me?"

"Loud and clear, Sarge. Guess what, Sarge. There are some

holes here at about shoulder height."

Mags started jogging. "Don't touch any of them. I'll be right there." With those words, she saw Deeks's light disappear.

"Deeks, Deeks, come in." She was speaking through her implant and ran. Then she used her brains. "Teve, find out what happened to him."

For reasons that she had not bothered to read up on, the native had night vision and could see in the darkness. It was only a moment before Teve spoke to her in her implant.

"Better hurry."

She was already running at full speed and knew her heavy breathing was probably carrying through the dark room. She had no choice but to keep moving, letting her penlight give her a place to step.

She had a pain in her ribs by the time she caught sight of the wall that was Teve and could stop. She bent with hands on her knees to ease the pain behind her ribs and get air into her body. At last, she stood upright and pulled her penlight loose. She twisted the front and let it spread to a large square light on the floor.

It revealed a hole. She flashed the light upward and Deeks was right. There was a bank of holes at about shoulder height in front of the hole.

She stepped as close as she felt safe and looked down. She didn't see Deeks's light. She scooted around to the other side, hoping to catch a glimpse of the flashlight. But she saw nothing but dark.

"Teve, with your eyes, can you see Deeks?" She slid back to allow the native to approach the hole.

He actually spread his legs over a corner and leaned down to look, but when he stepped back, he shook his head. "It is too far down, or the floor is painted black to blend into the darkness. If that is true, then he could be anywhere down there."

Leaning against the wall and letting her light shine on the square hole, she understood what she was seeing. A square panel had just slid back and under the side panel. She flashed her light at the side panel and could see where the second panel sat below the floor.

"I wonder how many bones I would break if I just jumped?" She was thinking out loud.

"Both legs if you even tuck and roll. Even with my strength, I would not try it."

She flashed her light over the bank of holes again and heard a noise. Turning the light down, she was just in time to see the floor panel move back into position. The floor was now complete with no proof that there was a hole beneath that neat fitting panel that was exactly like all the rest of the floor panels.

She spent the next twenty minutes to a half hour doing everything she could think of to open the panel. She swiped, pushed, and covered each hole. She used her light in different ways until her arms were tired.

She finally sat down beside that one panel, her back against the wall and gave her light to Teve to let him try everything. Nothing he did caused a change in the floor panel.

On the top floor, Scanlon, Thomlinson and Ski were also looking down a floor panel hole that had opened up and swallowed Aero.

"It looks like a chute." This came from Thomlinson.

"Can you see Aero?" Scanlon spoke as he leaned over the hole from a different angle.

Thomlinson shook his head. "Nope. It seems to take a gentle angle back in the direction we came from."

Ski looked at the holes on the wall behind the opening. "Do

you think his shoulder brushed one of these?"

Scanlon looked at Ski. "You can't reach him by standard contact?"

"Nope. It doesn't make sense. Someone hold on to my legs." Ski instructed as he lay down and stuck his head into the hole to contact Aero. "Nothing, pull me back."

"Loo." Thomlinson got attention as he was unwrapping a spool of very fine wire. "You guys hold on to this end and lower me down the chute."

He handed them the roller and hooked one end of the wire to his belt. The roller contained what was called climber's wire that could hold up to two thousand pounds and needed a laser tool to cut it.

Scanlon held onto the handle of the roller and Tumbler held onto the other. With a nod to everyone, the trained climber slowly moved down into the chute.

Thomlinson used his back on one side and his boots on the other to control his slow downward movement. He was soon out of sight, but the roller was unloading at an even pace.

The men shifted around the square panel, Ski adding his support on the other side of Scanlon. Scanlon thought they had everything under control. There was plenty of length on the roll. He almost smiled as he thought they could lower Thomlinson all the way down to the first floor.

That was when the floor panel slid back into place, snapping the wire.

CHAPTER NINE

Deeks slowly woke up and decided not to move. His military and first aid training all kicked in at once. Not knowing what damage he had suffered or how many enemies might be around dictated no movement.

There were some lights on in the ceiling above him and the wall beside him. It was a strange light—a solid metal panel seemed to glow with a soft light. Lying on his back, he realized the ceiling was at least fifteen feet above him. That was quite a fall.

He slowly moved his head for two reasons. One would be to see if he had any damage to his head or neck and the other would be to discover if he was alone. Moving the head let him locate a wound to the back of his head that didn't seem to be too serious. He also seemed to be alone.

Lying still, he tested all the muscles in his body and thanked the manufacturer of the field suit. All the many units in it meant to protect from enemy fire had also protected him from a long fall.

He looked at the ceiling carefully and couldn't decide which panel had been open. They all fit together with neat seams. He thought about it a moment as he rolled onto his side away from the wall. It didn't matter which panel, because he had no way to climb up.

He took his time getting up and found his flashlight. It didn't survive the fall. His weapon, still strapped to his chest, was in fine working order, and he knew he had a small penlight in one of his pockets. He decided he would need it when he walked out of the lighted area he was in at the present. The rest of the room seemed to be as dark as the one above.

Now on his feet, he used his bare hands to investigate the wound on the back of his head. There was a small amount of blood, but it was scabbing over. He went into his med packet and brought out some ibuprofen for what he knew would turn into a headache. He chose the gel tabs and swallowed three.

He reached down and found his water reserve, taking a sip to clear the pills. Now that he was upright, he looked around. He tried his earbud but got no contact with any of his teammates or the ship.

"Fuck, I gotta' keep my hands away from those stupid holes." His voice had an echo in this section. "Okay, maybe another empty floor."

He took a few steps in the direction they had been heading on the floor above. When he moved, a few more panels glowed and the ones behind went dark. He stopped, then turned and went back to where he had fallen.

The light panels followed his movement. The ones near him glowed, and the others went dark.

"Okay, so I am going to have some light, but it won't stay on when I leave an area. This ship is a fucking crazy bin. To make it worse, here I am talking to myself. Why not, I can't hide, so even if an enemy hears me, they already see me. I am a walking target."

He hesitated a moment, then searched another pocket and came out with a marker. He drew on the wall the symbol that the sarge had drawn on the walls above. It was an arrow showing the direction he was moving in and the stair going up at the end of the arrow.

Now he started his strange march forward, lights on and lights off in a weird dance that copied his movements. He hoped they would also light up if someone else moved into the room.

Above him, Mags was again trying anything she could with the holes without standing on the panel. "I'm afraid that there has to be weight on the floor panel for it to open."

"I can be of service." Teve stepped up and stood with one foot in front of the panel and one on the other side. He then leaned a long arm over against the wall. He took his weight off the foot at the side and put it on the panel.

"I think I have about one hundred pounds on the panel. You try the holes."

Making sure she had a solid stance, Mags leaned forward and swiped at the holes in different ways. She waved up and down, then tried one hole at a time.

"Can you hold the position?" She knew he was unusually strong compared to most Earth people, but she had to admit to herself she hoped he would say he had to take a break.

"I'm fine, keep trying."

Damn, I hate this beast. She tried several combinations that she didn't think Deeks would even have done, but she still wanted to cover each hole. Finally, in anger, she moved her penlight over the holes without results.

"Okay, whatever Deeks did, I can't repeat. Our best bet is just going to the stairs and hoping he isn't too hurt to do the same thing."

Mags pulled out her marker, and without stepping on the panel, she drew a circle around the holes and above it drew a small round circle with a line at an angle thru it from eleven o'clock to five o'clock. This meant stop or danger or don't go. She drew the same circle and line much larger on the panel.

She walked around the panel, and above the next panel she drew the arrow and the stairs. Her stomach was cramping — she needed to get to Deeks or the rest of the team. The presence of this shape shifter near her was giving her the terror she was fighting to hide.

Teve had moved ahead, and she wasn't sure if that was good or bad. She didn't like the idea of him behind her in the dark. Yet on the other hand, she had no idea how far ahead of her he was in his silent way of moving.

Her mind wasn't working in its normal logical way, so she had lost track of time and distance. She should have marked and counted the panels as they walked past the wall. She touched the implant behind her ear to pull up the time and found out they had been in this construction for five and a half hours.

She knew she was confused, because she would have guessed it was a full day that they had been walking. They had been in different parts, and she still couldn't confirm whether it was a ship or a container. She also wasn't sure if it was uninhabited. She wondered if her teammates were just as confused.

Scanlon was confused and worried. He had allowed himself to get separated from members of his team. They were on what they assumed was the top floor of this ship, and it wasn't the control center. It was full of very impressive suits of modern-day war armor for beings that were larger than the average Earth human male.

He, Tumbler and Ski were now heading towards what he hoped was the front of the ship and maybe steps going down, so maybe he could contact Thomlinson and Aero.

He looked around as they wiggled one full panel away from the wall. There was something in the metal of those panels that could cut through the climbing wire that could withstand almost anything except a laser blast.

He looked at Ski as the soldier was constantly working his

equipment to get through to the other members on their ear-buds or the ship. Ski was the best with contacts, so they let him work. As for Tumbler, that marine was a top sharp-shooter.

Tumbler had lots of weapons, but his special long barreled Raytheon Special R25 was a modified type of rifle that could send out many rounds, fast and accurate.

All three of them were in top shape and could jog at this pace for several miles. In fact, it was part of their training schedule any time they were down on a base.

After an hour, Scanlon called a rest. The end of the room was so far away that it was impossible for the eye to register.

Scanlon's voice had a slight echo. "Tumbler, use one of your best scopes and see if you can spot the end of this room."

He had nothing to say to Ski, as the marine was too busy being frustrated with his equipment and the silence from eve-ryone except the three of them.

"Okay guys, relax your muscles and refresh your body's proteins." He pulled some bars from a leg pocket. Times had changed and field rations actually tasted good to the tongue. He had a choice to pull out a bottle or tap the tube that con-tained his backup water. He sat down on a heel and was just working a bottle out when the first pellet shot past him and slammed into the wall.

"Shields up." That was all he had time to say as he rolled and hit his arm button to give him some questionable protec-tion. There was nothing to hide behind, so they needed to get near the hanging armor.

The three marines separated, each taking a different stance or roll as pellets or bullets continued to slam past them into the wall. Ski groaned but still kept moving. The shield had slowed the hit and his suit armor had kept the pellet from penetration. He would still have a bruise, and if one hit in the chest, he could have a broken rib.

By this time, Tumbler had leaped to scramble up one of the suspended units and over the top of a hanging form to find an area to shoot.

He spoke quietly in the earbud. "Loo, I can see it. It looks like a small square robot about waist high. It has three weapons sticking out of the front, and it is coming fast."

With that, he fired quickly. He threw in heavier ammo and ran out a full load again while his two buddies tried to duck and make their way to the hanging shapes that would give them some refuge.

Scanlon move sideways, then jerked the other direction as he saw a body back shatter into pieces in front of him. Okay, those were serious bullets coming at his men.

Tumbler pulled a couple of grenades and sent them out through the launcher and at last he got some good results. The little box exploded.

Scanlon stopped moving at the sound of the explosion and looked around to check on his men. Tumbler was grinning as he hung onto the top of one of the black forms. Ski was slowly stopping a roll he was making under a couple of black forms.

"I think my grenades killed it, Boss." Tumbler nodded as he came down, cradling his weapon.

Looking down at his marine, Scanlon raised a question. "You and your equipment okay, Ski?"

"I got a bruise so I can get a ribbon. But I need to take some time to check everything else to see that nothing got hit."

He looked around. "Ski, move over here where you can watch us. Sit down and check your equipment. Tumbler and I are going to look at that angry little box."

Ski moved to where he could see down the wall in both directions and between the hanging bodies to watch the aisle that had a crooked standing metal box.

Tumbler went straight down the same aisle that the box was in, while Scanlon took one aisle over to move in connection with his partner. They didn't have far to go, maybe thirty feet.

Ski shook his head, thinking how close the little killing machine had to be to get to them. This was bad news. He had to wonder how many more of those little boxes were around, hidden behind all those hanging black shapes.

Tumbler was now kneeling in front of the robot. "Boss, I didn't kill this machine all by myself. My grenade triggered some of its own explosives, and that blew the bottom out."

Coming out from the next aisle, Scanlon looked down at the top and the three muzzles projecting from the front. "So, did our movement set it off, or did someone tell it to attack us?"

"Can't say for sure. Even worse, I can't tell you if this is the only one out here."

CHAPTER TEN

A ero thought the chute would never end. He felt it twist and turn back to move in a different direction. The problem was that the fall was so steep he couldn't find any way to get control of his movement.

The chute seemed to be made of some slick seamless material that was semi-transparent. There were points in the drop where there was nothing but darkness, and then there would be a distant white light glowing through the round walls.

He tried pushing with his boots and with his hands, but there was nothing to hang onto or slow him down. Fortunately, it seemed he didn't speed up either. His fingers felt the sides of the chute, and it seemed to be made of tiny beads. They rolled him downward in a steady motion.

He worked his helmet on and pulled his face shield down. He pulled his weapon up in a ready position and tucked his legs up. Now all he could do was hope that the chute didn't end by throwing him out into space. Earth had a policy of not polluting the universe, as they took their trash home. Better still, they produced items that could be consumed or left little trash.

He was thinking of his off-ship suit lying by the entrance where they had boarded the ship when the crazy ride ended and he was dropped into a free fall to be caught by a pile of debris.

With his knees up and gripping his weapon, he hit and rolled over a supply of whatever had been tossed down the chute. A puff of dust flew up as he hit and rolled. Coming out of his roll, he tried to find something steady to stand on, but kept moving as things kept shifting under his boots.

The fine powder in the air settled as he finally found a lower area that seemed solid and free of garbage. He called it garbage in his mind, as he decided that the area he was in had collected unwanted items. Garbage.

Now that he had taken the joy ride down, he decided he was at the bottom of the ship. *Wow, top to bottom in one fast trip.* He snarled at the thought and went through the different channels to see if he could contact anyone. Nothing but static came through on his earbud.

Aero moved away from the chute in case more of the garbage coming down might have something heavy, like the metal slabs on the ground. He was grateful that the walls were all glowing. It didn't make sense to have the garbage dump lit up, so he treaded carefully and kept his weapon ready. There might be a garbage man down here.

There was only one way to go. Where he had fallen seemed to be the collection point. There were some tracks built into the floor and what looked like a couple of empty large carts sitting on the tracks.

Aero moved over slowly to look into the first cart and saw only small scraps of metal on the bottom. He would stay close to these carts, as they would give him something to hide behind. He might need it now as he heard something coming down the chute.

Taking a good spot behind the first cart, he propped his weapon on the top lip of the cart and watched a dark shape drop down into the pile, kicking up a ball of dust.

When the figure rolled out the same manner as he had, Aero realized another marine had followed him down the chute. He lowered his weapon and moved around the cart to help whoever had come after him.

By the time he got to the marine, Thomlinson was standing

up and coughing. Unlike Aero, Thomlinson had not put his helmet on and the dust was choking him.

"Hey, Thomlinson, move this way and you can get out of the dust. It settles pretty fast."

Still coughing, Thomlinson reached out, nodded, and joined Aero on the firm floor.

Aero pulled out some water for Thomlinson. "Thanks for coming down with me."

Thomlinson gave a short laugh. He held up the line that was still attached to his belt. "Don't get too emotional. It was a mistake. I was coming down on my wire when it got cut by something."

He unhooked the wire and rolled it up. "We might as well save however much followed me. I got whipped by it several times on the way down."

"Fuck, I guess that means no one else will be joining us." Aero kneeled down on a heel and brought his weapon back in readiness.

"Right. I think the floor panel closed and cut my wire. It takes a lot to cut one of these." Thomlinson had the end of the wire in his gloved hand. It was a clean cut.

"Are you okay for a walk?" Aero spoke over his shoulder as he continued spotting.

Thomlinson looked around. "It looks like we have to walk in the wrong direction from what the Boss directed the team up above. No choice, though, as this dump room is a dead end. I'm fine, Aero. Let's see if we can find a way out of here. I'll be your six."

Deeks didn't like it being by himself. He was not hearing anyone on his earbuds as he tried to contact his teammates. He appreciated that the lights turned on as he moved, but he was uncomfortable that they turned off behind him.

Basically, he was in a giant dark room with a spotlight on him if someone wanted to shoot at him. He took some precautions.

He put his helmet on and pulled down the face shield. He then turned on the body shield and put his weapon in ready, against his chest. This all was cumbersome, but he walked further for a few minutes. Then he heard a swishing sound.

"Fuck, is that another R2D2?" He turned to face the darkness of the immense room and saw something off In the distance.

Like his own motion, a distant square can on rollers was evidently moving toward him, causing the lights to illuminate it as it moved. Like him, the lights went off behind it when it moved forward.

Here Deeks was in a macabre dance, on a stage with a spotlight only on him and his partner. Then a pellet flew past him and this was a dance of death. R2D2 was shooting at him, and he had nowhere to hide.

He did a tuck and roll, hoping he could beat the reaction of the lights and be in the dark, if only for a few seconds. Although he seemed faster than the moving trashcan, he was not faster than the lights.

He needed to charge the machine shooting at him, dodging back and forth. He could destroy the machine now that he knew the machine's speed. His problem was, if he left the wall, how could he find his way back?

His next roll was a little slow as he was thinking through his problem and he felt the pain as a bullet punched through his shield at his upper arm. It was one of the weaker points in both his armor and the shield, and the pellet went straight through to slam the wall that was six feet behind him.

He did a quick jump back and then realized he had an answer to one of his problems. He saw a couple of red spots on the floor as he dodged left again. His wound was leaking. If he let the drops go, he wouldn't lose that much blood and he would have a trail of breadcrumbs to follow out of the woods if he could kill the big bad witch.

According to his timer, it had taken him just over an hour to kill the square shooter. Deeks was now sitting, leaning against the crumpled device as he repaired the hole in his arm. The bright lights shining down on him were a help in looking at the arm that had suffered a straight through shot.

He used the items as instructed in one of several packets in the med pouch. Now the blood drops had ceased, and he flexed the muscles to make sure he had full use of that arm.

He was lucky in two ways. The wound was minor, and the lights in this area would let him see an approaching enemy. Of course, the enemy could see him, so it worked both ways. He got up and kicked the crumpled box one more time.

He turned away when the side he had kicked on the box popped open. Deeks might be trained as a first-class field marine, but his specialty was in rare metals. This machine was full of open wires made from what he would swear were osmium and iridium.

Who has enough of those rare brittle metals to use them as open wires in an aggressive robot? Who owns this ship? These questions ran through Deeks's head as he pulled a handful of wires to take as samples. He would need to test them later to confirm his diagnosis, but he was sure of his guess. That was the main reason why they'd put him in the field.

He adjusted his clothes, adjusted his weapon, and followed his blood drops back to the wall, then came back and walked a few feet away from what he thought was dangerous drop panels when he heard the swishing sound and saw the lights come on in the distance.

He sighed, wondering how much energy he had in him to fight another battle. Deeks shrugged and remembered this was what marines did in the field. He could tell he had a few minutes, so he pulled out a protein bar. After the bar, he drank a full bottle of water and then took a stance with his weapon on alert.

Deeks was a little worried. Either this robot was further away, or he was having some trouble with his eyesight in this strange ship. Finally, he had something to gage the size of the new robot as it got to the crumpled shooter. It was small and almost flat against the floor.

It made several trips around the shooter and then started following his blood drops. Now he understood what was happening. This thing was cleaning the floor. It was almost like the unit he had back home in his apartment.

His bet was that the one at home was not full of very expensive wiring and this one would be worth a king's ransom on Earth's market. He decided to move on, watching the cleaning bot. He had to suppose that some type of trash collector would come along to remove the destroyed shooter.

Watching the cleaning bot slowed his progress, and he was surprised to see the little guy head straight back to the shooter. He was too far away to see what happened, but evidently the little guy hooked onto the shooter as it moved away, towing the damaged box.

Deeks stopped to watch as the light got further and further away until it was a mere dot. He gave up and turned to continue his trek to what he hoped was a stairway to join his team.

CHAPTER ELEVEN

Mags had finally found a pace that she could travel at with her penlight. She could just see the heel of one of Teve's boots as he made each step. She knew he had matched his pace to hers, as he was capable of a much faster and sustained march.

She was thinking of this thing they were inside of and still trying to determine if she was right and it was some type of repository, or if Scanlon's guess was correct and it was a spaceship.

The beast's low voice broke into her thoughts.

"Something is coming."

"Where?" Mags swung her light around.

"Sergeant. I know this is hard, but trust me. Sit down and turn off your light. Unfortunately, the light will draw it to you."

Oh damn, could she sit here in the dark with a shape shifter? But he was right. She was the only bright spot in the room. She sat down and turned off the light. Then she thought everyone knew where she had been when she turned the light off. She got on her hands and knees and crawled a few feet away.

At last, sitting in a stiff position, gripping her penlight, she tried to slow her breathing. She listened for Teve, then smiled to herself. Of course she wouldn't hear his movements. He had spent his whole life creeping through jungles, hiding from the Trio troops who had invaded his home world.

She heard something. It was a swishing noise that was far

off in the room. She stared into the darkness, then off at an angle she saw a faint blue light wink. Mags heard a couple of pellets slam into the wall near where she had been standing before she turned the light off.

She stretched out flat on the floor, deciding the lower she was, the less of a target she made for anything shooting in her direction. Now she heard a lot of noise. It was as if something was being slammed against the floor, over and over.

At last she could hear a screeching sound, as if metal was being scraped over metal. It continued, and Mags soon realized it was coming closer.

She heard Teve's voice over the irritating sound. "You can turn your light on now."

Okay, I hate this guy. Mags sat up and turned her light on and moved it around. At last, she caught sight of a large box like the one that had been a rescue box. This one had what looked like rifle barrels sticking out of the front top.

"What do you think it is, a special weapon?" Mags looked at the broken box.

"My guess is it is some protection device that is triggered by the movement of an individual that is not of the ship." Teve pushed it closer. "Can you tell anything from its design?"

Mags put her penlight on full spread to let the beam cover the whole crumpled box and moved close to it as Teve stepped back. In the light, she saw only the back of his boots. It dawned on her he was facing away from her.

She had to ask. "Are you expecting company?"

Teve's voice was almost a whisper. "Just being careful. Let me know if you need any help."

Being a little more comfortable with the beast a few steps away, she looked at the crumpled box. Her guess was that with his strength and speed, he had picked it up and slammed it on the floor. He'd probably slammed it several times to do this much damage.

She could see the mangled barrels, and behind them through a bent seam, were some strange items that had to be bullets. She wanted some of those but couldn't ply the seam further open.

She pulled out a knife and pushed it into the seam with no results. She wasn't strong enough even with the knife to pry the seam further open. She hated to do the obvious, but she had to use the best tool.

"Teve, I need you to pry this top off." By this time, she was kneeling at the box, and before she could move, he was leaning over her to look at the top. Unable to do anything, she just pointed at the seam. "Can you pry this open?"

She held up her knife, but he didn't take it. Instead, as she watched, he allowed his hand to change and long fat dangerous claws appeared on the ends of his hairy fingers.

He inserted a couple of claws and flipped the whole top off in one pull.

She couldn't help but stammer. "You have claws."

Teve turned the hand in her light to let her see it for another moment. "Yes, I can bring them out when needed. In sex, some females find them exciting when I drag them down their body gently."

It took her a moment to absorb the full effect of his words, and then she was shocked at the reaction of her body. Her stomach tightened as her core heated and her thighs clinched, all in a sexual response. Mags sucked in a deep breath, grateful he had moved away to take his position again as guard.

It took her only a moment to berate herself. *What the hell is wrong with you? Was it something he sent out? Maybe some testosterone scent that came from him?* She had smelled him. Different from the marines who had the odor of the latest shaving gel and ordinary sweat, he had smelled like the jungle, rich dark earth and damp plants in a clean male with musk from animals mixed into his body. She got up on shaky legs and pulled out some bullets.

She didn't care what it was or what had happened to her body. She was a scientist, and she could get control of herself. She tucked the bullets into a pocket into her pants and backed away from the unit.

"Uh, Teve, I think we should move on. Are you seeing or hearing anything else?"

He moved out of the light, but she heard his low voice in front of her. "We will continue. Do you want to leave a mark for the team?"

Damn, she just wasn't thinking. "Yes, give me a moment." She took the marker and wrote an OK and then the arrow and stairs, all at the edge of the dead shooter. With that done, she stood up, narrowed her light beam, and turned it toward the floor to find his boots.

They had gone for another ten minutes when Teve spoke softly for her to turn off the light and get down. By this time, she didn't hesitate to do what he whispered.

Lying on the strange metal floor in the dark, she now heard a shuffling and dragging sound behind them. Turning her head sideways, she had her ear against the floor and could hear the reverberation through the metal.

"You can get up. It is a cleaning bot retrieving the damaged shooter."

Mags heard his low voice right next to her and, with a reflex, she immediately rolled away. She turned her light on as she looked to see him down on one heel next to where she had been lying on her stomach. Even down in a crouch, he was still a big man. She took one more roll before rising on a knee and then standing.

He was already up and moving away as she turned her light around. "Wait. Did you say there is a cleaning robot out there taking care of the damaged shooter?"

"We should keep moving. Yes, a cleaning bot. It is small

but seems to be powerful. It hooked onto the box and just started pulling it back the way the box came."

She flashed her light up ahead until she caught him and lowered it to the back of his boots. She jogged a bit to catch up and then slowed down to his pace. She had a bunch of questions, but it might be better to walk without the noise of talking.

Scanlon had his team on the move. He was concerned about a possible broken rib on Ski. The expert on contacts was working on trying everything he could think of to contact anyone. So far Ski was frustrated, as he couldn't reach anyone. He reported it had to be the metal in the walls and floor. Still, he was not about to give up.

Tumbler was roaming several steps ahead of them. He was scouting out for any more trouble from robots that could shoot at them. Tumbler held his special weapon against his chest like a baby. In his nimble way, he would sometimes jump up on the nearest hanging body wrapped armor to search for trouble.

The three of them were marines, and they worked together as a field team should. Scanlon might have been separated from some of his marines, but the ones with him were determined to help him get everyone back together again. That was what a team did, no man left behind.

Ski looked up from his gear as he walked. "Boss, I am fine, and I think we need to move faster. Thanks for the considerations."

"Affirmative." Scanlon nodded. "We have wasted another hour here." They started at a jog and headed in the direction that everyone had chosen.

All they could hope was that they would reach a set of stairs at the end of this long trek, because they were going to push themselves to reach that goal.

On what they considered the bottom floor, Tomlinson and Aero were going in the wrong direction. They had no choice, since the room that the chute dumped them down into had only one exit.

They followed the tracks that had two carts that were basically empty except for traces of left over junk. There was plenty of light, but no sign of doors or exits points.

"Wait." Thomlinson turned as he spoke over his shoulder. "Let's see if this last cart can be pushed."

Aero stood and looked at him for a moment. "What's your idea?"

"Well, we can use it as a shield, and maybe it will help us when we get to the end of the tracks."

Aero nodded and had just grabbed onto the cart when they both ducked, as they heard a loud crash back in the dump room. They waited for a moment, but nothing happened except for a small puff of dust coming their way.

"I think someone threw away some trash." Aero pointed to the dust in the distance.

Thomlinson pushed the cart, and it moved easily. "Think we should check it out?"

"Well, it might be another teammate." Aero started back and Thomlinson left the cart to follow.

It turned out to be a waste of time, as the trash was a crumpled square box.

Aero spit. "Just garbage, let's go push your cart."

The cart moved with very little noise on the smooth tracks until they came to a wall. The tracks seemed to run right through the barrier. The two marines looked at each other and nodded. They pushed the cart up to the wall, and instead of stopping, the wall opened and they followed the cart through into the next room.

Here, both of them stepped back from the cart when a red light spread out from above, scanning the inside of the cart. It turned off and nothing happened.

"Must be scanning for items. What do you think, do we keep pushing?" Aero looked up at the ceiling.

Thomlinson pointed. "How about climbing? You know that is my specialty."

What he was walking towards was a built-in ladder in the wall of the room. There was a small panel above it that was large enough for the marines to fit through. The question would be if they could get it open.

Thomlinson got ready, checking his pocket for the wire he had kept. "Let me go up first. This is my strong point. If I can get the door open, I can send the wire down for you to hook on for safety."

With this, Tomlinson was moving up the wall, using his arms and hands mostly on the wide indented divides. At the top, he lodged one foot into a step and held on with a hand in the top step to allow his free hand to swipe over the holes. It worked, as the square panel moved aside under the ceiling.

After boosting himself onto the next floor and staying on his stomach to search for any danger, he felt it was safe enough to get up. He climbed down the climbing wire. He didn't watch Aero climb up, as he was checking his surroundings for safety. He did constantly take up the slack of the wire to protect his teammate as Aero climbed the awkwardly spaced indented steps.

Once Aero was on the floor beside him, Thomlinson breathed a sigh of relief. He heard the panel slide shut. "Those panels can cut through my climbing wire."

"I'm glad you waited until I was up here to tell me that detail. Any sign of the enemy or teammates?"

Thomlinson shook his head, watching the horizon.

"Nothing moving so far."

Suddenly, the entire immense area they were in went black. All lights went out.

"My big flash got destroyed, but I have a penlight." Aero whispered.

"I have a large flash, but do we really want to draw that type of attention to us?" Thomlinson said as he dug out the smaller light.

They both put their lights on narrow-beam and made their way to the wall that they decided was the back or side of the ship. It had to be the opposite of the wall that they had first been walking on with the team.

"This should still lead to the same place. When we get to the front, even if there are stairs, let's follow the wall to the inside to see if we can find stairs in the same area that our teammates are looking."

The two healthy, well-trained marines jogged and were making good time along the wall until they heard a noise and their lights were on a wall that opened to allow a small square box on treads roll out in front of them in the dark.

CHAPTER TWELVE

The box rotated, and pellets flew into the air at the two men. They rolled and separated. One light was left on the floor, pointing at the small box. It wasn't necessary, as the flash from the muzzles pointed it out in the darkroom.

Both men had their shields on as they attacked back at the box. It did not seem to move, just rotating between the two men, shooting at one first and then the other.

Aero shouted out an idea. "Stay down low, it seems to not shoot towards the floor. But see if you can keep its attention so I can get close enough for a grenade."

"Aye, sir." Thomlinson spread out on the floor, slithering like a snake, then waved his weapon up with something tied to it.

The box turned and let go with a barrage of pellets tearing through whatever was tied to the waving weapon. Aero crouched and moved several steps closer with the grenade ready to explode on contact. He tossed it with precise aim and dropped back to cover his head.

The grenade explosion hurt their ears as they both were close, but the shooting stopped. The light on the floor had been jolted aside, so Thomlinson grabbed for it and put it on wide beam to illuminate the box.

The box was on its side, one side crumpled in. It was missing one tread that was in pieces around on the floor. Both men got up and moved to examine the box closer.

"It's a robot of some type." Aero said as he looked at the wiring and plates that showed through a broken plate on one side.

"I wonder if it is just programed to be triggered by our presence, or if someone sent it after us." Thomlinson poked at it.

"Well, it doesn't matter. We need to get going. We'd better put a few steps between each of us to protect us in case another one comes out."

In a ready mode that left their mind more active, they again started jogging. Like a bunch of ants needing to return to the nest, they had the push to find and join their team.

Deeks had a headache, and his shoulder hurt way down to his fingers. He had treated the wound and it had quit bleeding, but he hesitated to take any pain relief. He felt he needed his brain clear and his feet in control. He put a topical pad on the wound to help. Still, the deeper pain increased, and he had to ignore it as he walked on toward what he hoped was a stairwell.

He decided he wasn't thinking as he was trained, so he slowed down and while still moving with the lights keeping him covered, he pulled out a couple protein bars. He finished the bars and was taking a long drink of water when the lights over him lit up a wall ahead of him.

He stopped moving. He put away the water and went into readiness mode, listening for any sound. He heard nothing. He took a step closer to the wall and saw that right at shoulder height was a palm panel with a series of holes.

"Fuck." He was mumbling out loud to himself. He moved along the wall about ten paces and there was another palm panel with holes. "Fuck, fuck."

He began to walk, letting the lights overhead turn on with his movements and knowing the ones behind him were turning off as he got out of motion range. Every ten feet, there was a palm panel with holes, exact duplicates of one another.

He finally stopped and went down on a heel, rubbing his arm. He had to make a decision. He got up and approached the wall, standing on a panel beside one with a palm panel. He reached over and covered the holes with his hand. The panel under that section rolled open to show a dark hole.

Deeks stepped back and waited. It took a couple of minutes, and the floor panel closed. He walked down a few more panels and chose another one at random. Standing at the side, he covered the holes and drew his arm back as the floor rose. It disappeared into the ceiling that had opened at the same time.

He looked down, and there was a floor panel in place. He tried it again and watch all the action. Sure enough, as soon as the floor panel began to raise, the ceiling panel slid to one side. After the floor panel moved upward, another panel also moved upward to fit into the floor. But the ceiling slid back into place, so the moving panel was still going up.

He made a decision to try to ride up. "No pain, no gain. Fuck, did I say that?" He rubbed his arm as he stood for a moment looking at the holes.

He tried one more idea. He reached from the side and covered all but the bottom hole. His idea was right. The floor panel moved to the ceiling, and a new panel covered the floor.

So, if he covered them all, the lift would go up a long way. Cover all but one or two, and it would only go a stop or maybe two.

Taking a deep breath and a solid stance on the panel, he covered the entire panel. He immediately went down on one heel as the panel moved upward. He had guessed correctly, for the panel moved through tall floors, one after the other.

Deeks was grateful that he had partially kneeled, as this gave him better stability. There was no wall once the panel cleared the last room. He was just floating upward through the center of large, empty rooms. Some were dark, some even had large containers in them, and some were bright with lights, but entirely empty.

At last the panel stopped as if it were a floor panel in a room full of hanging black containers that were shaped like large bodies. Deeks was back up where the rest of his team should be located.

He moved off the panel and still went down on a knee for safety's sake. He then tried his comm unit.

"Team 1, this is Dee Four, come back."

There was a screech, and then he heard a voice. "God dammit, Deeks, where the hell are you?"

"Oh shit, Ski. I am so glad to hear your voice. I am on my knees somewhere in the middle of these hanging suits. Is there any danger around?"

Ski clicked his comm. "I think we took care of the hostile."

Deeks smiled. He loved this team. "Aye sir, so how do I find you guys?"

There was a click and then a wait. He knew the team was working out details. Finally, he heard Ski giving him instructions. It was simple.

He climbed up on top of one of the body suits and made himself comfortable on the top so that he could look around over everything. It was fairly easy, even with his sore arm. It didn't take him long to see that off in the distance, Tumbler waving at him. The sharpshooter was an idiot, standing with legs spread on two of the body hangers.

Ski spoke thru the comm. "Tumbler says your best choice is just to come to the front and jog over to us. You should see us and we'll wait for you. Are you in good shape?"

"I have a wound on my upper shoulder, but it won't slow me down to get with you guys. Just cover my back for any more shooting boxes.

Suddenly, just the thoughts of getting back with his team

seemed to kill the pain in his arm, and he climbed down from his perch. He still was a trained marine in a difficult position, so he stooped to check below the hanging cases near him for safety.

He took a deep breath and started jogging towards what he was calling the front of this line of black hanging rows. Breathing heavily, he finally made it to the front and stopped before stepping out into the open. He took a field crouch and slowly stuck his head out, looking in both directions.

There was nothing close, so he eased out but stayed away from the wall by at least two panels. In the direction he wanted to go, he saw a couple of shapes in military field uniforms.

He couldn't resist the need to speed up. He stood up and began a good jog, heading toward the waiting men. He felt such a relief after being in the dark that he promised he would never put his hands in front of those holes again.

Several guys were waving at him, and he raised his weapon over his head. He should slow down, but after what he had been through, he needed the contact of his team. He was careful to avoid those panels near the wall. It was more important to reach the people than slip and fall down again.

One last wave of his weapon over his head and a big smile froze him in mid-step as bullets slammed into his side. They tore through his body, through above and below his vest, and a couple went all the way through him. He heard the noise of them slamming against the wall.

He was falling forward onto his face as blackness closed around him again. He had one last thought. "So close, fuck."

CHAPTER THIRTEEN

With the echoes of shots ringing out in the surrounding metal, Scanlon and Ski were flat on the floor and Tumbler made one leap to take his special weapon up high. He almost slipped as he was scooting up again on one of the hanging black armors.

"I have negative target, how about you, Tumbler?"

"Negative. I see Deeks down, not moving."

The noise was still loud and bullets were flying out from between the aisles. The wall over Deeks was being pitted with pellets banging into it with a noise to deafen the best of ears.

Tumbler clicked. "Lieutenant, I'm going over the top to get closer."

"Affirmative. Ski, let's try to move over under the hanging items and then scoot forward slowly."

Ski did two clicks to acknowledge, and they both slithered like snakes. Ski came out in front of him and tapped his boot, prompting him to move forward with a shake. This was a tactic they had all been taught in their initial training when crawling under the old-fashioned barbed wire.

It was an effective way to move without raising any part of the body. Spreading the legs and pulling a knee forward to push it against the floor would move the body in the direction you wanted.

At last the bullets quit pounding, but there was still the sound of something that reminded them of triggers and barrels working. All of this went on with their own noise that seemed like forever. They wanted to reach their fallen teammate, but they needed to stay alive and in one piece.

After what seemed like too much time, Scanlon heard the click in his ear from Tumbler.

"Boss, I got it. It is another shooting box. It is far enough away from Deeks, so I am dropping a grenade. Be ready."

The two men on the floor covered their heads and still heard the explosion.

There was another click. "Enemy eliminated."

Scanlon got up. "Full alert. Hard to tell how many of the shooters are up here. Let's see if we can help Deeks."

Tumbler clicked. "I'm covering from up here. I will bounce from aisle to aisle to watch for enemy approach."

Scanlon thought it was a good idea. "Ski, let's still stay close to the first armors hanging in each row. We have no clue what is tripping these boxes off and sending them after us in blasting mode."

All three of them wanted to run to their downed teammate, but they knew of the tricks the enemy could play. It was necessary to move slowly and surely until one of them reached the rare metal expert that had been part of their team for so long.

At last Ski and Scanlon were close enough to have one of them go to Deeks. Ski was in front, so from a nod from Scanlon, he got on all fours and crawled over to his buddy. A quick check told him what he knew but was hoping he was wrong about. Deeks was dead.

"Fuck Loo, he died as bullets tore through him. He never turned his shield on, and his armor protection didn't stop some of these bullets." Ski looked back at his who was standing with his back to Ski to watch for any more enemies. Ski could also see Tumbler moving carefully from the top of one aisle to the next, taking positions to see down each opening.

Scanlon glanced back with a look of real anger showing in his eyes. "I hate to do this, but we can't take him with us. Do a field closure."

Ski looked around at his teammate lying in blood on the floor. "Ah fuck, Boss, isn't there another choice? I don't want a cleaning bot taking him away."

A field closure meant that you took everything important out of the dead marine's pockets and pulled his tag. You plunged a finder on him and you pushed the one-man sleeping enclosure that would seal the body from head to toe.

Tumbler spoke from one of his spots. "So, cleaning bots pull everything away?"

No one answered as Tumbler moved again. "I have an idea. We open one of these holders, throw out the armor on the floor, and put Deeks inside. We will find him by his signal later."

Taking the wires from Deeks's pocket and some of the newer bullets, they finally closed up the sleeping unit, then struggled to get him into the hanging black holder. The cloth had dropped to the floor, so they had to pull the cloth back up and drape it over Deeks's sleeping shelter. The shelter was hooked to metal where the armor had been hanging. It looked a little smaller than the rest of the armor hanging in the rows, but it was done.

They left the armor on the floor, pushing it over to where Deeks had fallen.

"Okay guys, we have lost a good marine and a lot of time. Let's move and stay alert. We can't jog with the shield on, but we need to be more alert than we were in the past."

Not knowing what the rest of the team was doing, Mags thought about her own problem. She was Sergeant Margaret Bloom, a member of the Marine Corps, which was a part of the United Countries under her own USA in the development of the military in space.

She'd been lured into the military with promises of free labs and supplies and the opportunity to work with Professor Dunn. Dunn was the leader in the field of mental ministration and matching cognitive controls to circuit stimulators. In other words, and making it seem simple, letting the brain turn a switch off or on without the body touching anything.

Like almost everyone in the military, with possibly the exception of First Lt. Scanlon, no one bothered to read the small print when they signed that long paper as they enlisted. The Marine Corps was all volunteers.

Here she was, out in space, so far away from her lab that her home star was not even in the heavens above her. She was in an unknown floating container, built by undetermined beings and in the company of a mythical shape shifter. *Oh, wait, to be politically correct, the natives of his jungle world are called human modifiers. My life sucks, all because of that small print.*

"We are coming to a barrier." Teve's whispery voice interrupted her feel-sorry time.

Flashing her light up and past him, she saw a pile or barricade blocking their direction. Mags broadened her light, and it only showed her that the pile reached the ceiling and stretched from the wall out into the room as far as her light would shine.

Mags thought for a moment before speaking to Teve. "Uh, Teve, do you have a title, or are you in the Marine Corps?"

Teve looked at her, and the light reflected off his beautiful blue-green eyes. Then she shuddered as she could imagine the change into a jungle beast with those eyes looking for its next meal.

He stepped out of the light. "You have a lot of mixed emotions about Veld and my kind, don't you, Sarge?"

She wasn't sure if it was better to have him in the light or in the dark. "What is Veld?"

"That is the name of my planet. You call it something else, and no, I am not part of your Marines. My full name and title is just Teve. In my language and on my world, there is a lot of understanding attached to the word that is my name."

She flashed back to the barricade to change the subject and get her mind back on business. "So, how big is this mess and what is it? Why didn't the little cleaners get this out of here? What is its purpose?"

His chuckle surprised her—she didn't know he could laugh.

"My answer to all your questions is the same. At this time, I don't know."

She let her flashlight roam over the strange barricade. Walking over closer, she decided it all looked like the same material, just different sizes and different colors. She took time to put on her gloves and reached out to touch a piece that was sticking out at an angle. It was soft and gave, almost like the foam used in some cushions and mattresses.

"Since I can see in the dark, perhaps I should go out and see how far this pile of soft discards is stacked." Teve spoke in his whisper, but he was so close she fought not to jump.

"Good idea." Mostly, Mags thought it would be good if he just would step back away from her. At last, she felt him step back, and then he was gone. He made no sound, and there was no slapping of feet on the metal floor and no heavy breathing. Yeah, he was a jungle beast inside an alien vessel.

She did what she hated to do and sat down, turning out her penlight. The shooters were less likely to find her without the light, and Teve would find her in the dark.

At last, she heard his voice. His whisper was far enough away to give her warning. "Sergeant, it goes farther than I thought it wise to leave you. I didn't think it wise for us to be separated for too long a period."

She turned her light back on and spread the light. It wasn't as big as the ones the other teammates carried. "So, I guess we do some mountain climbing."

Teve pushed against the soft material with one foot. "It won't be easy. It will be like climbing sand. I don't like the idea of disappearing down into smothering soft pillow material. Any better idea?"

She thought for a moment, then hunted through her pockets. "Do you think it might burn?"

He threw a small piece near her, and she used a separate small unit that could light items. It was actually electric but would do the job. She wadded a piece of paper next to what he had thrown over to her and lit the paper first, then stepped back to watch. The foam-like material bubbled, but it also sent up a lot of smoke. Mags decided it made more smoke than what one would expect from the small piece.

"Burning is not a good idea," she muttered, and she waved a hand to keep the acid smoke away from her eyes. She turned her penlight on the barricade again.

"Do you think we can dig a hole through that pile?"

He pulled out a few large pieces and tossed them aside, further than she could have tossed even one of the pieces. Within seconds, the pile shifted, and it seemed like there were now more pieces in front of them.

Teve moved directly into her light. "What next, intuitive female?"

She turned the light away from his large body to study the wall beside them. The barricade was stuffed to the top and stretched outward. Unfortunately, that led her to believe it was very wide or even covered the area up to the end of this room.

"I refuse to stand here and wait for shooters that maybe just once you can't outrun." She looked up at the wall again. "I think we try to climb next to the wall. If we slid down into the soft piles, we try to use the wall to work back up to the top. I think we need to cover our faces with our glasses and something over our nose and mouth."

CHAPTER FOURTEEN

At first, Mags found the climbing interesting and the back wall a solid reminder to move forward. She was afraid she was going to sink into the pieces of foam, and it wasn't long before she stepped on something that gave sideways and she was going down.

She leaned into the wall and let it steady her as her legs went with the pieces. She felt her weapon come up to find an enemy and realized she had to remain calm. She gave the weapon an instruction to return to her chest.

She struggled to bring her feet back under her, but the soft pieces just shifted like quicksand, only larger. It was all meant to cause panic in the dark and the need to get air, as pieces pushed against all parts of her body.

Suddenly, something strong clamped around her ankle.

"Sarge, can you hear me? I have your leg."

Oh shit, answer him. "I hear you."

"Good, let me push you upward. Keep your hand on the wall." His voice was in her ear pod but also inside her. Then she felt him moving her upward. She stiffened her leg and slid her hand against the wall. The pieces were moving away, past her head and shoulders, and she shoved something that snagged on her weapon out of her way.

"Female, do you swim?"

She heard his voice but was confused by the words as she struggled against the false sense of smothering. She was getting plenty of air. It was just the darkness and the foam pushing against her.

"Can you hear me, do you swim?" His voice seemed very close, and she now understood his words. Was he just trying to distract her?

"Yes, of course." Where was he? He no longer had hold of her ankle. She had her hand on the wall and held still for a moment to rest and release more of her panic.

"Use the same motions. Swim through these pieces. Try it."

She felt his hand on her lower back and to get away from him, she left her weapon and pushed her hand forward, then swung it wide with her palm open.

It worked, as she pushed some pieces away, and the motion pulled her forward. She stayed close to the wall but tried the motion with both arms and moved further. *Ok, this might work.* In her next attempt, she added a kick of her feet to shoot forward in what she thought was several feet. She ran into a problem on her next try, as a large piece hung up on her weapon.

"Uh, Teve. It's working, but my weapon catches on some things." She pulled her weapon free and tried to turn it under her arm. She had pulled her knees up and curled her back. In the tucked position, she became aware she was not moving. She was not sinking into the pile, she was just part of it, held in that one place.

"Teve, I can rest in one place and not sink. I need this rest for a moment." She took a breath through her face covering and then a few more to help her body. She felt warmth—Teve had used his strong, strange muscles to swim beside her.

She might not see him in this dark cocoon, but she felt him. He gave off heat like her favorite electric pad back home. Then she jerked and straightened out, causing her to move with the debris. It was when she remembered he wasn't a heating pad, but an alien able to transform into a large impervious deadly animal.

She heard his whispery voice. "I smell fear from you."

Mags thought it was best to cover up her feelings that she thought might be unfounded. "It is just the dark and being buried in pillows."

She moved to get room, to swim again, but she stopped when he had her hand.

"Sergeant Margaret Bloom, my brain is the same person regardless of the shape of this body. That is why the Wisoo people are hunting for the gene. Tell me, as you swim, what is the real reason that your rocker attachment doesn't work all the time?"

He let go of her and she pushed hard with her knees together like a mermaid. She gained several feet upward and forward. She finally decided to answer him just to keep her mind busy, as she continued the swimming motions.

"In the lab, the rocker attachment worked every time. So we put it on a hundred military weapons and ask for a hundred volunteers. We explained all they had to do was put on a special headset and tell the rifle what to do."

She swam for a few more strokes and then snorted before continuing. "It failed seventy-two percent of the time."

She pulled with her arms and knew he was waiting for her to continue. "We pulled in a hundred civilian volunteers, rebuilt some new weapons, and it failed sixty-four percent of the time. Then someone got the idea that instead of tearing down the failed weapons, to pass them to a couple of people that had passed the test. The failed weapons worked in the right hands."

"So, you discovered that the error was not with the rocker attachment." His whisper was not a question.

Mags answered it as she thought about the lab's problems. "Some people didn't believe. If they didn't believe the brain could operate the weapon, then it wouldn't."

She heard him very close by. "If the Trios do not understand that to modify is to believe, they will never succeed.

Their mind set will never let them believe. They think like most of your military type. They will always look for a switch to turn on, not a brain belief."

Again, Mags stopped and relaxed, becoming one more piece of debris. She was thinking what he was saying. She wondered what it would take to convince the military to let a screening be set up to find and build a team that believed?

She knew it would work, because it worked for her. There had to be some clues in some people, like their religion or gambling, or maybe how many friends they had that would lead to a screening test. Mags knew that Professor Dunn and the entire staff on the rocker project knew where the problem was, with the operators and not the rocker units.

With that impressive team working together, they should be able to come up with a good and easy screening test. They could use the background of the people who already could operate the rockers and go from there.

The modifier was so close, she stopped again as he whispered. "You have an amazing mind. It works all the time in different directions. Too bad the military put you in danger."

"Can you read my thoughts?" Now she was using up too much energy, trying to swim hard to move away from Teve. Slowing down as her common sense took over, she realized his strength could pass her easily.

"No, my many gifts do not involve mind reading. You project your emotions. Not just to me, but to anyone around you. I watch the marines respond to you. Most of their reactions are due to you and how you project your feelings. You are an interesting female."

His words gave her mind something to chew on as she worked her body harder than just walking. She was wondering if her quick temper got her into extra trouble because it hit others in the face faster than she meant.

She thought about her last tangle with a guy or friend. It

was a mix as they worked together and they couldn't figure out if it was a friendship or more, at least she had not made a determination.

It was good to have something to think about beside the big alien beside her in this pile of pillows. *Damn. Wait, think, I am supposed to be a lab rat. Are we going in the wrong direction?*

"Teve, can you hear me?"

The answer came immediately. "I am next to you."

She was determined not to let his presence get her off her decision and idea.

"We are going the wrong way. We need to go to the floor and find a panel with holes." She shifted in the soft debris and let her body sink as her weight and the gravity of the craft pulled her down. This was what they had been resisting the whole time they had entered the pile, and now she let nature take its course.

"My feet are on the floor." His whispery voice came through.

She gasped as he had his hand around her ankle, pulling her down through the black piles of softness. She reached out with her left hand to push a large piece away and she felt the wall.

"Teve, I found the wall. Can you see it?"

There was a low chuckle. "Little one, I can see in the dark, but not through things. I will move right behind you to touch the wall as well. Can you turn your light on?"

She decided that was a good idea since he had let go of her and she felt the floor under one foot. She shuffled the other to move something out of the way and then had both feet steady. Keeping her one hand on the wall, she reached for her penlight and turned it on.

It was a funny red blur, as it was up against a piece of something that was red in color. "Teve, some of these items have color. I'm pushing my body against the wall."

The voice this time was right behind her and not in her

implant. He had moved up against her. She fought the reaction of her body and went into the mantra she'd taught herself for her first-time use of her weapon. *Control is in the mind, and the mind controls the body.* She said it twice.

Her voice shook as she spoke. "Are you close so that you can see me?"

"I prefer to go down with you when you get a panel open. That is what you intend to do, correct?"

Mags couldn't help but smile. He was as smart as she was, but he just had a different training background. She wondered if they had laboratories on Veld. It was also strange that she was calling it by his native name and not the star chart number.

She used the foot nearest to the wall to move forward. It was the best to move the soft debris away from the wall. With her light in the hand on the wall now, she even saw some breaks in the piles, as some of the different shapes held openings.

Getting her mind on her mission, she pushed ahead, letting the light shine on the wall in limited amounts. Once or twice, Teve's long arm came around her to pull a large item out of the way, and then she hit payday.

Her little light was encircling a small square pad with holes in it. She stepped in front of it, forcing as many soft items away as possible. Suddenly Teve was up against her with a muscular arm around her waist.

"What the hell are you doing?"

"Going where you go." His breath was in her ear.

She swiped the buttons quickly, partly to get away from the debris and mostly to get out of the encircling arms of Teve. The floor panel slid open, and they fell through together with some smaller pieces.

They twisted in the air, and Teve was under her as they fell into a large room that was bright with lights. They hit and rolled, and even with Teve protecting her, she still had the air knocked from her lungs.

Gasping, Mags cleared her eyes and rolled off the big body that had kept her body safe. She wondered how many bones were broken in his body and stared at the beast. He was the full beast. He had shifted as they plunged down at least twenty feet to the floor.

He rolled in the opposite direction away from her, and she was having more trouble getting air and getting her heart to work. He was huge as he rose. In his human form, he was about seven feet tall. As a beast, he must be at least nine feet tall and at least five feet wide across the shoulders.

Crawling backwards awkwardly on her hands behind her with her feet pushing, she could only stare at the almost animal body that was all bulging muscles with each leg wider than her body.

The hair on his head was long and wild as it spread out over his shoulders, thick like a long lion's mane. His skin stretched over the body with not an ounce of fat. It had a warm color of tan and sun even on the back of his hands, which were almost as large as her head. The hands ended in the large claws that she had seen before. Now, attached to the whole towering beast, they made him look formidable.

He turned and looked at her as she was still spider- crawling away. His face had changed, longer and fuller, with a fierce look in every way except for his eyes.

They were still the blue-green eyes to Teve.

CHAPTER FIFTEEN

Three strong and deadly marines were jogging in the dark in an alien ship, separated from their team and very unhappy. Thomlinson, Ski and Scanlon were in top shape and could jog for miles without food and water or stopping.

Their adrenalin was high after they'd killed a shooter and they were on alert, ready for any other attack. They were running without their shields on, but they had their full equipment ready, and in the old days, they would have said everything was *locked and loaded.*

They wasted no effort on words as they pissed in bottles as they moved. If a shooter found them, it would find a fast-moving, difficult target. They scattered, taking turns leading and staying at least ten feet apart as they kept the same pace, step by fast step.

But even the strongest runners must stop if they reached a barrier.

"What the fuck is this?" Scanlon asked as he flashed a light on the wall while he let his body pull in air to relax.

Ski talked within his earbud as he moved away. "Seems to be a long wall, Boss. Any ideas?"

Tumbler was moving in the other direction. "Hey, Lieutenant, here is one of those pads with the holes. It is set beside a panel or door and is about two inches deeper in the wall. I ain't touching it."

The other two marines joined him, and with all their lights on the inset panel, they examined it with no shadows.

Scanlon decided to be the one to step on the panel in front

of the inset. "If I go down, jump and come with me."

He leaned in and looked at the inset panel that was about nine feet tall and four feet wide. "We need our scientist sergeant to help us with her intuition. Judging by the size of the door, the builders must have been larger than us as they constructed it. Let's hope that's as big as they come. Now our problem is, do the holes open the door or the panel beneath my feet?"

Tumbler shifted his weapon as he added his thoughts. "Maybe you should step back, Boss. What happens if the door swings this way?"

"I think everything slides sideways," added Ski as he shifted his light to the panel with the holes. "The floor panel went sideways."

"True." Scanlon continued to stand before the door. "Guys, get right behind me on the floor panel. We are going to stay together no matter what happens."

Three very-heavily field-dressed marines got body to body on the one panel as Scanlon reached a hand toward the holes at one side. Behind him, he heard Ski mumble.

"I will shoot one of you that tells anyone about me being the icing in the middle."

Both his teammates chuckled as Scanlon swiped the holes. They all got quiet as the door slid sideways into the wall, opening the way into another room.

Scanlon gave the order as he moved. "Go and spread."

The marines took an offensive protective position, facing in three directions. They heard the door close behind them and they moved carefully forward, watching for small square cans on rollers that could shoot deadly bullets.

There were three quiet voices with the word "Clear" in their earbuds, and the men didn't relax, but they stood up to get a better look around.

"So, there is our regular wall." Ski was closest to that side, and he just eased over to the wall they had been following.

Scanlon nodded. "Okay, Ski, stay near the wall. I will move out ahead. Tumbler, cover our asses. Now let's make up for lost time. I want my team back together, and I don't want to lose another marine."

So here they were again. They were three strong trained marines, jogging across a distant area in top shape.

"Hey, Aero, how long have we been in here?" Thomlinson asked around his protein bar.

Areo was about twenty feet ahead and standing watch. They were taking turns to allow bladder relief and food intake breaks as each man watched for the other.

"My watch says about eight hours now. I can actually see another wall up ahead, but there seems to be some type of large, dark opening."

"Dark, sure. No lights seems to be a pattern with this ship. Okay, I'm fine. Let's move."

Thanks to their training, they could go on for more than one day without sleep. They would not be out here if they had not passed that part of the training. Now they just headed at the proper speed towards the dark hole in the distance ahead.

Two hours later, they slowed to approach the opening carefully. Thomlinson fished out his large light, and the first thing they did was check the wall all around the dark opening for any palm size square that would hold the holes. There was nothing on the walls framing the opening and no holes.

The opening was about thirty feet by twenty feet, and it was dark except for some of the light from the area they were in that reflected on nothing.

Thomlinson stepped close to shine his light while Aero covered his back. "Buddy, you aren't going to believe it, but we found the stairs."

Aero backed up, trying to watch for the shooters, but also wanting to see inside the black hole. Thomlinson's light reflected a very wide set of steps going up and down.

Thomlinson swung his big light around and then looked at Aero. "Do you have any cleaning nets? We need to make sure there are no traps in this area."

Pulling the little bomb from one of his pants pockets, he tossed a net up the steps. The strings spread up in the air and across to the wide walls. The strings finally settled down in pretty colors onto the steps and nothing blew up.

Aero nodded. "So I guess we have a long climb up to meet the lieutenant. You first, and I will cover the rear with my penlight."

They were moving up the steps slowly when Thomlinson spoke in his earbud. "At least the rolling shooters can't climb. Still, they might have some other surprise, so just be careful."

The steps were not hard to climb, but when they reached the next floor, the room was dark. Thomlinson flashed his light into the room, and they both froze. There must be fifteen or twenty of the rolling shooters all lined up and facing forward towards the wall.

Thomlinson made a motion for stealth and turned his light off. In the dark, they quietly moved up the stairs past the opening that contained the shooters. Using the inside wall as a guide, they continued up the steps for another twenty minutes.

At last, they saw light coming in above them from another opening that had to be from a lit room. They moved slowly, not wanting to walk into another group of shooters.

They came up only far enough for their heads to peer over the edge of the bottom of the opening. It was a large open area, just like the ones that they had seen before. There were no shooters and nothing to disturb their view.

By this time, they still had enough surprises to take caution as the rule and they took a few more steps up to get a better view of a room to make sure it was empty.

"Why would idiots build this ship with these big, empty areas?" Areo was peering over his partner's shoulder as he spoke softly.

Thomlinson inclined his head. "Maybe the sarge is right. It isn't a ship, but a container with shooters to protect its contents."

"Hey, there is something moving out there."

Thomlinson brought up his weapon and looked through the sights. "It is two beings. They are too far away to see what or who they are, but they are bipedal. At least one is up and one is down in a crawling position."

Aero moved cautiously onto a higher step and pulled up his weapon, but his gun sight wasn't as good as Thomlinson's. "Could they be one of ours?"

"Well, I think we need to be careful. We also need to get more info. We aren't on the top floor, but some of our guys could have climbed down a floor or two and could be in trouble." Thomlinson mumbled as he watched the action in the far distance.

CHAPTER SIXTEEN

Aero nudged his partner. "I have an idea. If they are one of ours, maybe the earbuds will work."

He clicked and announced clear and plain. "Team One, please reply. Team One, anyone who can hear, report back."

Mags was still moving backwards with her butt on the floor. She had her hands behind her on the floor and her knees bent with her feet down in what she'd called a spider crawl, when they were kids. She needed to turn over and get up and run, but she didn't want to turn her back on the big animal in front of her.

He hadn't moved and made no sound once he stood up to his full height. On the fall down from the floor above, he had changed from a big male to a bigger beast and he had landed under her, taking the full brunt of the fall.

There were a dozen questions running through her head as she scampered backwards in the silly position. *How soon could he change back? Did he recognize her in this form? When would he become violent?*

Panic had adrenaline pouring through her body, confusing the words coming into her implant. At first, it took a moment for her to understand someone was talking to her through her implant. A voice was coming in clear, as if the person was standing next to her.

She quit moving, sat up on her butt and listened to the words.

"Team One, please reply. Team One, anyone who can hear, report back."

Touching behind her ear, she spoke through her implant. "This is Sergeant Bloom. Can you hear me?"

There was a click. "Hey, Sarge, this is Aero and Thomlinson. I think we see you, but you are really far away. It looks like there is someone else with you."

Looking over at the beast that had not moved, Mags answered through the contact. "It's Teve, who has shifted into the beast's form. He isn't saying anything."

There was a click, and Aero was talking. "Sarge, the Veldans can't talk in the modified form. He is fine, he just needs time to adapt and make sure there is no danger and then he will change back. Give him some time."

She fought to keep alarm from her voice. "Aero, where are you? Were you able to discover a way to talk through the floors?"

This time, she heard Thomlinson's voice. "We found the stairs, Sarge. We think it best if we wait here for you. Can you see the large square black hole in the wall? It is in the direction we were all walking when we started out, and Aero and I are sitting here on steps going up and down with only our flashlights."

"Yah Sarge, we will cover your back from any shooters as you jog over here. I figure it will take you most of an hour." Aero assured her he was a good marine.

Getting up carefully and watching the big beast, Mags took her eyes off him long enough to look into the distance. She was trying to see the dark spot Aero was talking from that signified the stairs. The problem was that the walls and the floor and ceiling were all made from the same material and the same color, and she didn't realize there was a wall in the distance.

What she saw was a small black rectangle in the remoteness of this area. It was hard to judge the range or length in a room that was all the same color, with no markers or pilings.

Well, there had been some foam debris that had fallen through when she and Teve went down as the panel opened.

"Hello, Aero." Mags activated her implant. "What about the beast if I start in your direction?"

"Damn Sarge, he is still Teve. He could be here in half your time, but I guess he will cover your back as you jog. I think you should get out of there before a shooter comes out with all barrels roaring." Aero's voice had a bit of urgency in it now.

From the looks of the small size of the black rectangle, it was going to be a long jog. Now Mags didn't look at the beast, just settled her MA12 into a comfortable position between her shoulders and straightened her clothes. She sighted her goal and jogged like they had taught her in basic training.

After a few minutes, her curiosity got away from her and she took a quick peek over her shoulder. There it was, about twenty feet directly behind her. The beast only took steps long enough to match her jogging.

She had a strange thought that the beast was impressive. It was the way a male lion or the great gray gorilla was impressive. You saw how strong and dangerous they were, all muscle under the skin and control in every movement. But they were all killers to survive. Did he kill to survive? He had destroyed the small metal shooter all by himself. Yes, he was a killer, but did he have more mastery and decision power than the gray gorilla?

Finding that she was jogging too fast, she made an effort to slow down to the right speed meant to cross the terrain without wearing out the body too fast. She looked up at the black mark ahead, and it seemed like it wasn't getting any closer.

It took another fifteen minutes for her stomach to cramp, and shortly after, for the first pain to hit her ribs. She tried to convince herself that she could shake it off. If she had counted the steps, it would only have been twenty more before the small ache turned into sharp enough to take her breath and cause her to stop.

She was stooping over, holding her waist, when things got worse. Two large hands picked her up, and the next thing she knew, she was hanging upside down, at least seven feet above the floor, over a wide shoulder.

Her eyes were looking down the back and seeing the tendons and muscles of a bare ass moving as the beast stretched out his long legs to cover the long space to the black rectangle.

Fighting her anxiety, she repeated her mantra instead of screaming. *Control is in the mind, and the mind controls the body.* Her problem, as she bounced on the wide shoulder, was that she was trying to control her body for a different reason. Her body wanted to leak urine, and she would not allow that humiliating action to soil her clothes.

Her other problem was the fact that she might throw up the protein bars she had eaten. She could imagine her sour vomit flowing down the hairy ass while the strong tanned legs below moved faster than she could comprehend.

With some blood going to her head and her whole system kicking up, she decided she had to get the attention of the beast.

"Teve, if you can understand me, I am getting sick, You must let me down." Mags pushed upward with her hands against his back.

"Teve, I can't hang in this direction any longer or I am going to throw up all over your back."

As quickly as he had grabbed her, he stopped. With a shift, he moved her down into his arms in front of his wide chest. He had an arm behind her back and the other under her legs, and he was running again.

Mags had no choice but to cradle her weapon in her crossed arms and rest her head against his hot body. The position was better, as his movements were just as fast, but smoother for her as her stomach and body settled down.

Rolling her eyes to the side, she saw the black rectangle that was now close enough to have some distinction. It was something to at least think about besides the large arms that were enfolding her as if she were a child.

She had heard that in this form the beast was almost bulletproof, yet his chest felt warm and soft against her cheek. Was the strength buried underneath in the unusual bones and muscles that formed in the change that happened?

Regardless of her situation, her scientific training and need to know poked its head up. She supposed it was why the Trios had taken some natives in the shifted form and cut them up with laser saws. She shivered at the thought and looked down at her weapon.

On the range at the testing site, she never thought about using it on any living being. Now she realized it would be easy to have the weapon take out the Trios if they were attacking the marines. Life changed, and you learned as you moved through to find there were many things you might complete.

Her mind was on the structure of the beast when she became aware he had thrown her down to the floor and in a way that she rolled. She turned over twice before she started to swear out loud at the animal when she heard the swishing noise.

She was flat on her stomach and could see the shooting can off in the far side of the room making its way toward them. The beast was already weaving from her, probably to draw the shooter to him and away from her.

Coming up on her elbows in the lying position, she let the MA12 slide into position between her hands and against her cheek. One look down the sight and she thought the kill and the gun let loose. Even at this vast distance, the weapon found its target and tore the can apart, sending it immediately onto its side. Pieces of metal exploded in small sections to slide across the floor.

Where she was lying, she raised her head and could see the beast skid to a stop and just take a moment to look at the demolished can. He was almost halfway to the little shooter and stood only a moment before turning and looking back.

Through her implant, she heard Aero.

"Great shooting Sarge. How do I get one of those MA12s?"

Mags got up slowly and smiled to herself. "You click your heels and believe, Mr. Trio Expert."

Thomlinson chuckled in the earbud. "I think she is yanking your chain. Hey, Sarge, that is also a great ride."

By this time, Teve was back by her side and looking off at the dark spot in the distance. She had a decision to make. He could cut the time down to half at his speed. She took a deep breath and looked up at him and settled her weapon and then raised an arm upward towards his high shoulder.

He just reached down and put her back in his cradled arms and began eating up the area that separated them from the other two marines.

CHAPTER SEVENTEEN

Tumbler spoke through the earbud to keep his voice quiet. He was on top of one of the hanging armors. "Boss, there is an end to the hanging armor coming up. I see about six more rows and then it just looks like the room is empty.

"Okay, let's take a short break." Scanlon also used the earbud. "Protein, water and relieve your bladders so that we can be prepared for whatever comes at us in a big, open space."

Up close to the last row, the marines did all the normal processes while still being on alert. Rest was not part of the process. Checking their weapons and equipment was necessary. Fifteen minutes and a reload meant they were up and jogging, taking turns at who was lead and who was middle position and who was six.

They were a half hour into their movement when the next shooter announced its approach by the sound of its rollers moving on the floor. It was far enough away to give them warning. Everyone went down flat and Ski took the position of snaking forward with an abundance of grenades.

Before he got close enough to toss the first grenade, the can began letting loose with bullets. Fortunately, the bullets were strafing over their prone bodies.

Being pinned down, there wasn't much Ski could do as the robot approached. The strange thing happened as the unit continued to shoot and roll forward. It ignored Ski lying on the floor.

Confused, Ski stayed without moving until the machine was several feet past him and he turned over and punched the button on the grenade. Using a sideways movement, he rolled the little round bomb across the floor and under the shooter. About two seconds later, just as the shooter was moving off the grenade at its normal speed, the blast threw it over on its side and it quit shooting.

The silence left ringing in everyone's ears.

"Good job, Ski." Scanlon cut through the ringing as he looked around for any other enemies.

Ski picked himself up and walking backwards, as he went to join his partners. "They aren't very smart, even if they are deadly."

"Yep, I would sure like to know what starts them up."

Tumbler added his thoughts. "Right. It all boils down to are they programed to react to unusual movements, or being directed by someone else on this craft?"

"They could be cats." Ski stated quietly as they moved in their standard direction.

"What the fuck are you talking about, Ski? Did you get a bump on the noggin?" Tumbler was now in the six position.

Scanlon let the men whisper. It made the time pass, and he knew they were active even while they spoke.

Ski explained his comment. "Cats were taken on the large tanker ships that traveled the Earth's seas before the tubes were put in underneath for transporting via the hyper loop engines. They loaded the ships with containers that came from many different companies and different countries. There were mice and rats and snakes that often survived the defoliants that were used, so cats could catch whatever moved before the ship landed at the next port."

Tumbler snorted. "So, these are rat catchers? The builders of this ship must have big rats. The shooters only shoot at three to four feet above the floor."

Scanlon stopped, and since he was leading, the other two held up in a defensive position. "If they are rat catchers and shooting in a specific area, then the builders have an enemy who is over three to four feet tall but has a weak spot within those parameters."

Two pairs of eyes looked for only a second before taking field action again. It was something to think about as they started jogging.

Ski was thinking of science fiction animals with iron bodies, but a head up at about three feet on top of a neck above the iron body. Tumbler was thinking of a tall android with its thinking parts in the middle.

Scanlon was just thinking of getting his team back together and finding some way to retrieve Deeks's body. It was at this point that his eyes caught a dark spot in the distance. It didn't seem to be any of the shooters coming towards them. It was something that wasn't moving and was still and long distance away.

"Tumbler, take that special weapon of yours and look through to that spot down there. See if your sight will bring up any details."

Scanlon took the six position as Tumbler kneeled and adjusted the long sight on his metal baby. "Rectangle. Dark and not showing any detail, but I would say it is an opening."

"Okay, with everything the same color, it's hard to measure distances. Tumbler, you stay lead and let's go. We have a target. Ski, watch for your rat catchers." Scanlon had a goal, and it was joining his team. If that dark spot might be another room or even better the stairs, they had to get to it fast.

As a trained officer, he was tracking out the routine. He would decide how many breaks, how many fast jogs and then down to steady jogging and then back up to fast. He hated to think of the area they were in, because it still looked like hours before they could get to that black spot.

"Enemy nine o'clock." Ski announced, as he was moving out at an angle, pulling out grenades. The other two men spread out and took positions on their stomachs. It was at this point that they saw that the first little shooter had a friend. A second duplicate copy shooter was following the first.

When they got within range, the cans began to shoot and the bullets slammed into the wall above the prone bodies of the marines.

"Spread out." Scanlon ordered.

Watching the two shooting robots, both Scanlon and Tumbler moved apart on the wall. A shooter turned toward Tumbler and the other turned toward Ski out on the floor.

Using only the earbud, Scanlon gave orders. "You guys stay low and keep them busy. I will move around and see what damage I can do." He moved out and crawled to the robot that was rolling toward Ski. Ski was the closest to a shooter and every time he moved, the can would turn on its rollers to face him, shooting over his prone body.

Scanlon took the time he needed to change out the rounds in his weapon to heavy metal piercing explosives. He then set it on automatic and held it tight against his shoulder as he allowed it to pour a group of the damaging shells into the robot. The can exploded along with its own shells.

Ski had to roll away to put the fire out that flared around him. Now both marines turned to help Tumbler, who faced a robot that was moving wherever he moved. The problem was that some bullets were ricocheting off the back wall and could be deadly to Tumbler.

Ski and both Scanlon rolled to shoot at the same time, destroying the second robot into pieces all over Tumbler. It would have taken a timer to decide which of the two men got up first to reach Tumbler. Then there were slaps on the backs as Tumbler was up, brushing off pieces of a robot.

Scanlon looked around and then down the wall at the black dot. "Let's get out of here."

They had run for another thirty to forty minutes with Ski

still on the outside. "Fuck Loo, enemy in numbers. I see three."

Scanlon pulled around and took a prone firing position. "Load up with heavy metal and kill them before they get close. I'm not fucking around with these guys anymore. Fire at will."

He heard his men loading and taking positions and Tumbler, who had the best weapon, let loose before either he or Ski had a good target. Through his sight, he caught the explosion of one rolling target and then Tumbler took out a second robot. Ski got his chance as the third shooter was over in front of him and his aim was true.

"Good shooting guys, I will save my shells for when needed. Up and running. They are increasing the numbers, so I figure the closer we get to that black opening, the better our chances."

They ran for another fifteen minutes, trying for as much speed as possible, when they heard the noise of rollers.

Tumbler was on the outside this time, but Scanlon looked over even as he asked, "How many?"

"Fifteen or more, Boss." Tumbler had his weapon out.

"Any suggestions, Loo?" Ski was loading two extra clips.

Scanlon also was reloading. "Yea, live through this and go find our team."

CHAPTER EIGHTEEN

Teve threw Mags on the floor again. He was learning, she thought, as the toss had a twist to it that let her roll across the surface without bruises. She came up and started looking around and saw the beast moving toward a shooter.

She twisted, her MA12 responding to her thoughts, and then she realized that there were now two shooters rolling across the floor. Without holding back, she gave the instruction, and the gun sent out two shots at one of the rolling shooters. As she believed it would, the robot stopped in its tracks with its top missing.

Teve, who was part way out on the floor toward the shooters, now stopped. She willed the MA12 at the next target and let loose with two more rounds, and before she even raised her head, the sound of the robot exploding could be heard in the area.

It only took the beast a few strides to return to the place where Mags was lying on her stomach. She had waited a moment longer to make sure there were no more shooter boxes. Teve was now kneeling beside her, so she turned and looked at the dark rectangle and then back at Teve.

Teve raised a large hand and tapped with one long claw on the barrel of her weapon.

"Can you understand me?" Mags looked at his blue-green eyes that were the only part that seemed to be human.

He tapped her weapon again.

"It doesn't work for everyone, Teve. We found out in the tests that you have to believe it will work before the mind will

99

work the weapon. Do you understand?" Mags wondered if Teve was really inside that immense body?

Still kneeling, he touched his one claw to his temple and nodded.

Mags wondered if he meant you had to believe in order to change into a beast. She didn't think she wanted to believe that much, as she wasn't ready to shift into something weird. But it could be the problem that was stopping the Trios in their underground laboratories.

As a scientist, her brain asked too many questions and out here in a war zone with a beast beside her was not the time to delve into these problems. Eventually, she would push to have all her queries answered.

Teve stood up, and in his usual speedy movements, Mags was up in his arms again. The difference this time was that she was trying to watch for rolling shooters, as she was moving across the floor at a faster pace than she could jog.

"Everything okay, Sarge?" Aero's voice came through her implant.

"Huh." Mags answered first as she was jarred by Teve. "They sent two after us. Teve is putting on some speed, because it looks like the hostiles are getting serious as we get close to your position."

Even with his faster pace, she could not hear his large feet against the floor. His natural way of traveling let him take long strides and still put his feet down without noise.

A beast that weighed almost two hundred and eighty pounds and was carrying a marine whose own weight was one hundred and sixty and carrying another sixty pounds of equipment—such a beast moved silently. His breathing was still even and smooth and almost imperceptible to her own ears that were so close. This body was a great work of nature or something inventive.

She had to study his planet when this was all over. As a lab rat, she had to understand how the gene pool could produce something this frightening among a small percentage of the natives that populated U231Z42.

Her mind was busy while another forty minutes went by with the bouncing in the beast's arms, so she was surprised when Teve sent her into a roll on the floor.

Damn, more rolling shooters. This was her thought as she took her best aiming position. She was right, but it was worse. There were a lot of rolling boxes coming at them from a distance.

She had never put the weapon on auto fire before, but now seemed like a good time to try that option. She reached down and pulled out a couple of full clips and put them beside her so that she could access them quickly. She sighed and went for the option and waited one more minute for the rolling enemy to be well in her sight. She killed as many as possible and the weapon let loose with a hail of ammo.

She hung on tight to the kick as it pumped back into her shoulder. It actually gave her a feeling of security to feel that thump. When the eye field screen warned *empty,* she ejected the clip and inserted the next and without looking at the rollers she shot, continued her sweep.

Within seconds, she was down at the end of the line and still had bullets left in the clip. She raised her head away from the weapon and saw the entire row of boxes down or bent. None were coming forward.

"Teve, if you understand me, maybe you should look at that line to make sure every one of those shooters is out of order. Please be careful."

She kept her position to cover the beast's back as he ran forward, examining the crumpled line. There were several boxes that were shooting, but the bullets were flying harmlessly either at the ceiling or at one of their own kind.

It took him only seconds to disable the last two shooters.

The silence left a heavy ringing in Mags's ears.

"Damn, Sarge, we need to get you in here before they send a battalion after you. I mean that weapon and you are doing great and both Aero and I are ready to click our heels. But we want you to get here in one piece first."

Sitting up now and refilling her clips with heavy ammo, Mags answered Thomlinson. "I agree, guys. I can't find my heart as I think I swallowed it. I will still let the beast — sorry, Teve, carry me, as he is the faster jogger. I am reloading and right now have a lot of ammo. I also have a load of grenades. Here comes my ride now."

Not wanting to waste any time, Mags stood up and raised an arm to let Teve pick her up and start his amazing run again. At least she was grateful to see that the black rectangle was closer and was now taking a definite shape against the far wall.

She ran the information she had about the rolling shooters in her mind, trying to find some answers. First of all, the rolling shooters were all the same height. They were about four feet tall, and their barrels came out at the top, making them shoot at a height of three and a half to four feet.

She decided the builder of the container had an enemy whose weak point was about at that same height. They were persistent but not very flexible with their movements or their decisions. She decided they were programed and not under the control of handlers.

That didn't discount the fact that maybe a handler triggered their release. The fact their number was increasing could also be automatic or by a controller. It wasn't good news either way.

If it was automatic, then the builders must have had some dangerous and persistent enemies. On the other hand, the enemy of the builders might be nothing more than an invasive animal or bug of unusual size. That thought meant such a thing would be dangerous to humans.

Mags's musing made the time pass, and they were getting close enough to recognize the rectangle as an opening. A marine inside flashed a light. She just about decided they might make it in the next twenty minutes at Teve's speed when she heard the rolling noise.

Teve sent her down on the ground and she took her shooter's position. It was the battalion coming for them. There was no way she could shoot all of them.

It took only a breath for an idea to hit her. "Teve, can you understand me?"

From her position on the floor, she looked over at his large body, ready to attack. Even as strong as he was, he would not survive this barrage. She saw his blue-green eyes on her face.

"Teve, they shoot only above three feet. Get down on your stomach and we will crawl to the stairwell. Hurry."

Within ten minutes, bullets were flying over their bodies as they pushed, pulled, and crawled their way across the floor. The back wall was being slammed by ricocheting metal. It reminded her of basic training in the Kentucky station, where they also used real bullets to teach every marine to keep their ass down as they crawled.

"Sarge, look on the ground, and you will see a small wire. Hold on to it, and I will pull you into our location. Do you understand?" The message was coming through her implant.

Looking ahead, Mags saw a thin metal wire on the pale floor a few feet in front of her. Looking back, she spoke over her shoulder to the beast.

"Teve, hold on to my boot. They are going to pull us into the hole." She felt his clawed hand clamp around her ankle.

Chapter Nineteen

Scanlon and his two teammates soon realized they were outnumbered, both by how many rolling shooters were approaching and also by how much ammunition the shooters had in the boxes.

The marines had one advantage. They could take a position on the floor as the strange robots continued to shoot above them. These robots were programed to shoot at a waist high position to any standing man and didn't seem to adjust their aiming height up or down.

The rollers had a limited and slow turning ability so that they could shoot in a different direction, but that didn't happen with all of them.

The team soon learned that destroying the rollers and tipping them over still allowed the extending barrels to send bullets.

"Grenade launchers or heavy ammo at their tops." Scanlon spoke too loud into his earbud as he moved on his stomach to avoid the shells pinging beside him from a tipped box that was still shooting.

Tumbler was doing what he did best, and with one shot each, had cleared a hole in the advancing boxes in front of his section. He was taking out each box with one explosive hit to the top, directly to the section where the barrel protruded. Tumbler had guessed correctly, as this had proved to be a weak section. His heavy, volatile cartridge struck true and blew the top off each box. He moved his long rifle on its tripod quickly to the next target and repeated the process. Stop a box, one deadly shot at a time.

His teammates were not as accurate, but still were having success with several shots from each man that took out one or two more of the advancing boxes. The smell of cordite and the noise were the atmosphere of war to the marines as they whittled away, piling a scrap yard of strange tin.

Tumbler took out the last two standing shooters. He then jumped up to run over to destroy the one robot lying on its side. It still threw out dangerous pellets until he threw in his own deadly type from his rifle at close contact.

The silence in the large room almost hurt their ears. Scanlon got up and spoke through the earbuds. "Everyone up, and we're going full out to the black spot on the horizon. No stopping for anything. Check your ammo. The next group will be bigger."

Scanlon was pleased that his men did as he asked. He had hand-picked this team several projects ago, and they had never let him down. Losing Deeks had hit them all hard, but there would be time for regrets later. For now, they had to make sure there were no more losses.

After checking on his own ammo, he was surprised at how much of his heavy stock was gone. He still had plenty of regular shells and a full load of grenades.

"Report on ammo, Ski first." Scanlon's voice jerked in the earbud as he ran.

"Boss, light on my heavy shells. Medium on my regular loads and lots of grenades. I have all the rest of the stuff that probably won't work on the box shooters."

Tumbler reported, "Still a good number of heavies and full load of regulars. I have a few grenades missing, but enough to be active. Like Ski, I have all the rest, but I don't think smoke will affect these rollers."

Both his men gave quiet reports with shaky voices as they continued their fast pace. Scanlon was point-man with

Tumbler at nine and Ski at six. They all had allowed themselves only one quick look at the black spot that was their destination. From then on, their entire focus was on full speed and staying alert for the next attack.

Sergeant Margaret Bloom had a very sore arm and no regrets, as she lay on her back in the dark stairway. She had been able to twist the climbing wire around her one free arm and keep her other hand on her equipment.

Thomlinson had slowly pulled her and Teve across the floor, under the constant fire of the rolling shooters. The pain of the wire biting into her arm even with the uniform protecting her increased with the weight of the beast, who was clamped to her ankle.

When they'd finally reached the entrance of the stairway, hands reached out to pull her into the steps. Teve let go of her ankle and rolled sideways to slide into the darkness below her.

While Tomlinson untangled her arm and worked to repair her injury, she listened to Aero talking to Teve in the dark behind them.

Aero's voice was just above a whisper. "Okay, big boy, ease off your change. Good, you are back to standard size."

She heard Teve's voice, the first time since he had shifted. "I'm fine. How is the sergeant?"

Thomlinson answered. "Sarge is okay. She has a pulled elbow joint I can cover with a pain shot and wrap." He looked at Mags. "You need to be careful with this arm, and remember, it will be weak."

She nodded as she heard Teve behind her. "I need something to cover important parts of my body. Any suggestions?"

Aero chuckled as he pulled out a large, thin blanket from one of their backpacks. "How about a diaper?"

Teve answered with a smile in his whispered voice. "We learned how to wrap clothes while in the jungles. I am proficient in finding a way of hiding my body with one piece of material."

Mags looked out at the line of shooters that had finally reached the wall and simply shut down. Now the amazing sight was small cleaning robots that rolled across the floor, attached themselves to the big shooters, and dragged them away.

Aero spoke over Mags's shoulder. "What do you think? Are they dragging them back to get them reloaded?"

"I have to admit, I'm confused by the whole thing. Whatever they were built to kill, it was three or four feet tall and didn't learn to duck down to the floor. This place is just crazy, and as a scientist I want to learn about it, but it seems to just give me more questions and no answers."

"So, Sarge, do we go up?" Thomlinson was flashing his penlight on the steps.

Mags nodded. "Yes, but we need to watch out for traps. If the builders expected something they needed to shoot at, then they might have thought it would get into their stairs. Let's use all your special equipment to make sure it's safe to go up. I also think we need to be extra careful when we come to the next floor opening.

I'm going to be a hindrance with this injured wing, so I'm going to stay in the middle and let you guys with the field experience to do your jobs."

There was a general agreement as the troop started up the first level of steps they'd cleared.

Feeling each riser with her foot, Mags was aware the steps were slightly higher than would be built for standard comfort on Earth stairs. She added this additional information to her inside notes. The builders had to be a little taller than standard Earth humans.

There was a hesitation as Thomlinson did something that created a flash. Mags had the left-over beams in her eyes after the sensor bomb cleared the next four steps. She wasn't sure why she was blinking her eyes, as they were all in a dark walled in section, but it was a natural reaction. She put her hand out to steady herself on the outside wall.

This wall was different to the touch. It felt like real metal with no paint or coating on it. As she moved up each step, she felt a seam and could tell where it actually interlocked within the next panel. These sections were apparently the outside of the ship, or at least not made to slide apart like the inner panels they'd had trouble with as they found holes and saw panels slide past one another.

The doorway above them was shedding light into the stairway, so they must be coming to another floor that was well lit. Thomlinson was still taking care of tossing items ahead on the opening that was wide and tall to ensure their safety.

Aero was the one who volunteered to ease up to have a look out the opening. Mags was staying near her wall and now could see the cold look of metal with the flat heads of bolts. Her eyes glanced up and got sight of Teve.

Talk about your Roman god, he almost took her breath away. He had a knot of the green blanket on one shoulder and then it draped down and, with a twist, went around his waist and gathered with a torn strip that made a skirt that covered just enough of him to make him legal.

As he stood with one strong leg up on a step, he looked as if he had posed for one of those old stone carvings that were still preserved in the Italian area of Earth. She had a definite thought that if one could forget what he was and where he came from, a lady could fall for such a statue. Unfortunately, Mags had the memory of his large animal hand with claws clamped around her ankle.

Aero reported. "Looks empty right now. It's a large room

with nothing in it. I bet if I step out, that within a few minutes a bunch of shooters will come rolling to greet me, guns making lots of noise."

Thomlinson, always a good marine, had shot out a clearing net and suddenly everyone was on alert. Something invisible in one place had cut some of the pretty thin ribbons as they spread out in the air. Instead of the strings flying from top to bottom and landing in pretty long strips all over the steps above them, there were sliced pieces.

Thomlinson barked a request to Aero. "I need fog."

Aero tossed a small round grenade that exploded without sound in the air and released a small cloud of blue smoke. There was nothing exposed by the smoke.

Mags had an idea. "It is a razor wire. Put something sticky and lightweight on it. There might be more on other stairs above."

The two marines searched their pockets carefully when Mags suddenly pulled out one of her small first aid packs. "Here, the bandage glue."

She passed the small automatic spray can to Thomlinson and he let loose a wide sweep of the glue. As it passed through the blue smoke and met the wire, it stuck with some tiny blue coating of smoke molecules.

There were now spots on the deadly wire that were visible.

"Are there any more?" Aero asked as he looked back into the room.

Thomlinson looked up the steps. "Not for the next fifteen or sixteen steps, as the trigger ribbons are smooth and all fell down."

Aero shook his head. "So, why a waist-high killer wire at this point?"

Mags had returned to her support on the back metal wall. Her eyes were interested in finding the connection that held up the wire, and she found one on each side. As she looked over this metal wall, beyond the wire, she saw the inset of a large area that could only be an entrance or door. Beyond it was a panel with holes.

"To protect from having anyone enter that door." Mags pointed at the door in the metal beyond the killer wire.

Everyone looked at her finger first and then at what she was indicating, the outline clearly showing in the light from the large room beyond the stairway.

The first one to ask was Thomlinson. "Damn, Sarge, does that lead to this ship's control room?"

She shook her head. "It is the wrong direction due to what we saw of the shape of this container from outside. Remember, it looked like we came in from one end. However, this was built by beings that had a different mind and perceived things from a viewpoint we might not understand yet."

Mags pointed at the wire. "We don't understand their protective stance at that particular level. Why is it that whatever they are trying to kill isn't smart enough to duck?"

"Maybe because they are too big." Teve's whispery voice came to all of them in the stairwell.

"Fuck. How do you kill something that is so big that even if it lies down, it is still over three feet high?" Aero looked carefully in the large lit room.

Thomlinson pointed at the blue segments now hanging in midair. "By putting up an invisible cutting wire that will slice it in half as it runs up the stairs to tear open that door."

"Why would it even be interested in that door?" Aero asked over his shoulder.

"Probably chasing someone." The short whisper from Teve made them all stop and think.

"We saw no traces of any big animals." Aero pointed out at the room he was searching.

Teve whispered again. "First, they might have been slaves that escaped, or animals that were being transported that got loose. There are a lot of possibilities. Remember the little cleaning bots, they would have taken away all traces of anything lying around."

Now they had a lot to think about, all because of Teve's words. His own experience on his world with the Trios taking his people captive and the vast amount of effort they spent to keep his warriors in cells. She had read that there was a way to keep the shifters from being able to return to their normal state.

It also said in the report that the Trios were extremely afraid of the natives in their expanded form and had to go to unusual methods to keep the shifters captive.

Mags looked over at Teve and wondered if he had some insight on what was happening in this large vessel.

Thomlinson looked at Mags. "So what do we do, Sarge? It's easy for us to get under the wire, and now that we are warned, we will watch for more of these killers. Do we go on up, or do we try the door?"

Aero added an opinion. "We could split up. Two of us could continue up to see if we can meet up with the lieutenant, and two of us can try going through the door. Whoever goes on up, if they meet the team, they can tell them about the door and come back down to this spot."

"I don't think it's a good idea to break us up. Too much has happened already, and the shooters are dangerous." Thomlinson was looking at the blue molecules floating on the wire that was mostly invisible.

Whatever they decided, her science node wanted to know what was behind that door. She knew there was a whole section beyond the wall that they had followed to get to these steps. There was a great chance this doorway would lead to an entrance to the next section beyond the wall and eventually to the other end of the interior.

Her busy mind kept thinking. That container could be a

control center at the other end of the capsule-shaped object they were exploring.

There were so many unanswered questions, and she was born and educated to seek answers. She knew she was going through that door.

CHAPTER TWENTY

Scanlon, Tumbler and Ski had one more battle to fight as they ran for the rectangle that was close enough now to be recognized. It was a dark room or entrance of some type, and they were determined to live to enter it.

They also were smart, well-trained men, and understood the weakness of the rolling robots. The shooters only let their bullets fly in a waist high level. They moved slowly and were easily taken out with one shot of a high-powered shell, or a well-placed grenade would destroy several.

They had learned a lot about the group of boxes that were approaching them across the floor. Scanlon yelled out orders. "Take out the ones at the front of the line in the direction we are heading. I don't want to crawl the whole way to that dark, small room. Start shooting, don't wait until they get close enough to shoot at us."

Ski was lobbing grenades, one at a time. He had a good arm and his first couple flings hit on the mark, the explosions taking out two or three boxes each. Unfortunately, there were boxes behind that moved forward to fill up the opening, keeping the line complete. They were moving past the damaged boxes.

"Fuck, Lieutenant, they won't make this easy." Ski spoke through his earbud to be heard over the noise.

Scanlon agreed. "Okay guys, on our bellies and crawl like you are six months old and see your mama's tits."

Even moving in the best way possible, with their equipment on their back or between their legs, their speed was slow, and the rolling boxes were coming. Damaging bullets were flying over them now as the boxes fired all three of their mounted barrels.

The men soon had to move away from the wall, as the bullets bouncing from the wall were dangerous. They were now crawling further out in the room. Now and then, one of them would stop to take a turn to take out a few boxes. Tumbler would use his expert shots to make a single strike at one top at a time, causing each hit to crumple a box.

Ski now had his grenade launcher attached to his weapon and was sending a grenade out every ten or twenty seconds. Scanlon was just strafing with heavy shells. He decided he would use up what he had and then go to whatever he had next in his arsenal.

Wondering why they were fighting this battle, Scanlon was on his stomach and loading his grenade launcher. He heard Tumbler, who was on a different tangent, taking out multiple targets.

"Hey. Look at the boxes running up against the pile I have down to the left of you."

Scanlon let loose with a grenade and, without looking at the results, he let his eyes go to the mess that Tumbler was pointing out with his red laser beam. There was a pile of boxes lying across each other, and the boxes behind them were just bumping against them and not moving forward. One box had run out of ammo and was still clicking away with loud noises, but no results.

Into the earbud he followed up on Tumbler's discovery. "Take out and add to the pile where Tumbler is shooting. We can get in front of that pile and maybe even break through and get behind these guys."

With this in mind, the three men inched toward the shooting rollers. They became attackers on their own instead of just lying down and trying to defend themselves. After all, they were marines.

The pile got longer, even though the sideline moved closer to the wall, shooting nonstop. The boxes were shooting at the wall and just wasting their ammo. Some of them ran out of pellets and continued to move and click through the barrels.

"Boss, the ones in the second row seem to have more ammo." Ski reported.

"Affirmative." That was Scanlon's only comment.

It was not important to target the boxes in the back of the pile they had built. There was a group of rollers bouncing against the pile and shooting as they tried to move forward against their temporary blockade.

A couple of more grenades, Tumbler's sure shots and even Ski's rapid fire took out the back row of the pile that they were building. The men ignored the rest of the rollers that were ignoring them. They still stayed on their stomachs and crawled to the pile.

Within, the crumpled metal boxes were still shooting straight up at the ceiling. They ignored the shooters and crawled over the pile.

Once behind the lines, they stood up and ran. It was full out running, to get to that black area before another line of rollers came out from wherever they erupted like good little killer robots.

Forty-five minutes of full-pace movement wearing complete field garments left them sweating, but still strong as adrenalin kept their legs moving.

At last, they leaned against the wall next to the opening. The light from their room showed a flat floor with no lights inside.

"Ski, throw a clearing net before we enter." Scanlon waited, nervous as they could hear the swish of the rollers and knew they had deadly hostiles on the way.

Ski sent in the ribbons and then, to be on the safe side, a

smoke release. "Clear, Boss."

Scanlon nodded. "Let's go."

Inside the area, with the reflection of the light from the room they left, they found what they were looking for, steps going down.

"Damn, we might find the rest of our team." Tumbler moved down.

"Easy, let's make sure it's safe." Scanlon wasn't about to lose anyone else after what they had just gone through to get to this stairway. "Let's take a break, get some rest as we have had a rough time. Take turns and I will start using my big light down the steps."

The light just showed a long row of steps that doubled back on itself at a landing. The guys all needed to be at their best before starting the next leg of their journey.

The argument was weird, as it wasn't about who was going with the sarge, but a guess of how many floors were between them and the rest of the team.

A brighter light on the stairs showed that there was a landing and that the stairs turned back to continue upward. There was an estimate of how high each room was and how long it took the elevator to travel up, passing dark and light rooms.

That discussion ended with no agreement on how many floors were in this monster and no one could agree who was going with the sarge.

At last Mags felt rested enough and frustrated, having let the men talk for as long as they wanted. She needed action. While someone was counting his ammo and another was counting steps, she got up and ducked under the blue molecules that showed the killer wire.

"Going somewhere, Sergeant?" The whisper of Teve drew everyone's attention to her. She was standing in front of the plate with the holes, having decided she had now decoded the process.

She decided a swipe downward was a complete command and would open the door and it would stay open for a time. Maybe it would have to be closed from the inside. Cover one hole, and it would open fast and close fast, perhaps if a monster were chasing you?

She spoke over her shoulder. "Aero, are you coming with me?"

Aero stood up and looked around at Thomlinson, and especially at Teve. "Sure, I guess. Why me?"

He ducked under the same place Mags had ducked and stood next to her, looking at her with a question in his eyes.

"You are used to working with aliens and alien effects. This door will probably lead us to an area that can go to the other side of that stupid wall. I believe we will see things built closer to the original beings that constructed this whole unit. Your years with the Trios and working with the natives of Teve's planet will give you some knowledge that will be helpful."

With that, she went to wave a hand across the panel. "Aero, you need to be alert, because we don't know what is on the other side. She then waved her hand downward and heard the door slide sideways.

The area beyond was dimly lit with pale blue light, but it was enough to give the two humans a comfortable sight into the narrow hallway.

Aero, being a marine and a gentleman, stepped into the hallway first, weapon at the ready. Mags followed and looked around to find that they were in a cul-de-sac. This hallway ended just beyond this doorway. They only had one way to go, and it was the direction she wanted to go beyond the wall.

"I should throw out a net." Aero was reaching into a pocket.

"Do what you want, but they know how to keep the big

animals out, so I don't think they set any traps in here." Mags looked at the plain metal that made up the walls, ceiling, and floor.

"Hey, Sarge, got any idea why this is here?" Aero was moving slowly forward in the dim light, weapon at ready, but able to see down the hallway that seemed to end at a double door built into the hallway.

"My guess, using human statistics, would be that we have reached a center of the construction and are now heading into the other section where the crew or members of the race that built this item would stay. I think we need to take extreme care." Mags was talking through her implant into his earbud.

"Hey, Sarge, don't scare me. I'm here to back you. I still hate those guys that dress up like clowns." There was a chuckle in Aero's low voice through the earbud.

She had an idea. "Aero, can you reach Thomlinson?" She listened when he stopped and heard Thomlinson answer the question.

"Hear you loud and clear," Thomlinson replied.

"Return. Clear. It seems while you are on the steps and we are inside this hallway, we can communicate. I feel better." Aero nodded at Mags, but then stopped as another voice broke into the earbud.

"Contact, this is Scanlon."

Through all their earbuds and Mags implants, they heard the voice of the lieutenant.

"Fuck, Boss, it's good to hear you. What is your location?" Thomlinson's voice was loud.

Scanlon's answer was quieter. "We're on the top floor, but just found the stairs. The sarge was right. There are steps going down. We just had a wicked battle with the rolling shooters but seem to be okay in this stairwell."

Aero added in at this point. "Boss, watch out. We just ran into an invisible wire waist high on the stairs that will cut through anything. We used the net and recognized where the ribbons got cut. It was still invisible in the fogger. Sarge had us spray out the sticky sealer from the med packs and some fog molecules stuck to the wire."

"Affirmative, we will be ready. You guys relax and wait there. It is easier for us to walk down. I am not sure how long it will take, but we will be in touch." Scanlon gave his orders.

"Oh, oh. We have a problem." Thomlinson's voice let Scanlon know he was not happy.

"Is someone hurt?"

Aero answered. "No, Loo. The sarge and I have separated from Thomlinson and Teve."

They heard his sigh through their earbuds. "I have had some bad news today, so I don't want any bullshit right now. What is going on, Sergeant?"

Mags knew it was her time to explain. "We found a door that I am sure leads to the other side of that damn wall. I believe it leads to where the crew or builders were at and not in this storage side. So Aero is going with me to see what we can discover. The good news is we seem to be able to stay in contact."

She stopped talking and motioned for Aero to continue down the hall.

Speaking in a low voice, Aero said, "I am announcing our movements. There are no traps and the light is a pale blue, easy to see. The hallway is bare metal with no coating. Ahead is a double door set with what seems to be clear panels like windows."

Aero was up against the doors, staying below the windows. Mags walked behind him, then slowly rose to peek through the edge of one clear panel.

The interior, what she could see of it, was also lit with the blue light, but it was a little brighter. In the distance, she could see some kind of equipment, but she couldn't identify anything.

Deciding it was safe to see more, she stood up to look down at the floor beyond the doors. "Aero, check out the areas you can see beyond the doors. I want to go in if it looks empty of anything that might be moving."

"Reporting the room has blue tinted lights, brighter than the hall. We can see something like equipment or controls about thirty feet away. Nothing is moving. I see an odd shaped bundle on the floor off to one side of the doors. Sarge is trying the doors to go inside."

Scanlon was trying to control his anger as he was allowing Tumbler to clear the way down the stairs. Having been fore-warned about the invisible killer wires, they could only travel so fast. He might be angry, but he wasn't stupid. He won't throw out all of their training and take any chances.

He listened to Aero's words as he stayed on the metal wall, away from the openings. He thought that when he got his hands on that Sergeant, she was going to be lucky to be a bare ass private, mopping floors in her own lab. That was, when she got out of the Lunar holding cells.

Tumbler announced it was safe to take the landing. It was a turn that was created on the steps to allow them to take the next group down. This led to another opening on a floor that was dark.

With no need to explore this floor, Scanlon gave the order to proceed downward carefully. They had big flashlights on the steps and high inner walls and it was one more turn that led to an open, lit floor but also a warning from Tumbler.

"Warning, net cut." This was from Tumbler's voice.

The other two marines threw their lights down on the strings and saw the pieces that had been cut, all lying to dec-orate the steps in colors.

Tumbler was digging out a med pack.

"Careful partner, don't get too close." Scanlon was concerned about something they couldn't see.

Ski moved down to the step that held Tumbler so they could work together. Ski waited until his partner was ready, then release the blue fog bomb. Tumbler sprayed a long up and down sweep with the sticky flesh repair.

Sure enough, a few molecules of blue stopped and held in the middle, about waist high above a step below them. Now that Tumbler had a target, he continued along that line with the sticky spray and blue molecules stuck to a long line. It wasn't a continuous line, as it was in small dashes, but it showed them where the wire was located.

CHAPTER TWENTY-ONE

They could see the bolts on each side that held the wire. The next thing their light reflected was an inset panel or the shape of a door on the inner wall.

"Damn. Boss, another door." Ski announced as he highlighted the square panel with holes.

"Yes, and the wire is to keep someone from coming in from that room over there." They all looked at the room Tumbler was showing them.

"What were the builders afraid of that they had to protect these side doors?" Ski looked around as he asked the question.

Scanlon shook his head. "They were carrying something in this container. It was built to hold something. Something so large that robots would need to kill it at three feet from the floor, even if they ducked. Something so dangerous that they left these invisible wires to keep them from entering these small doors if they escaped."

Ski brought his weapon up and looked carefully with his limited view into the room.

Scanlon spoke into the earbud. "Aero, how is it coming with you two? I don't suppose the sarge had stopped to wait for us."

Aero answered as he looked down. He understood that the scientist had put aside the sergeant and was looking at the bones of a large body covered in rotting cloth as if she were in a lab.

"The sarge thinks she has found what is left of one of the original builders of this ship or unit. She is examining its bones. It has been dead a long time. Nothing has been in this room for a long time."

Aero looked around and noticed some details in the sergeant's penlight. "Loo, there is a light coat of dust over everything and no footprints or anything that has disturbed it. We are only in about eight feet from the double doors. They opened with a push, and my clear net is mostly covered in the dust you would normally find in an area that had not been disturbed for years."

The sarge looked to be in science heaven. She first was taking photo clips of the body from all sides, trying to be careful not to disturb the dust. She was speaking quietly into a memo to record all her notes, noting the depth of the dust and the position of the body.

"It has fallen as if struck from behind. It had a humanoid configuration, she said, and with only the bones left, they appear to be a bit taller than Earth humans."

She paid no attention to Aero as he slowly approached the equipment. It seemed to be set up like a control panel or working site. He wasn't too worried about any enemy, as the dust proved that no one had come into this area for a very long time.

The lieutenant spoke in in his ear. "Don't get careless, Aero."

"Right, Boss. Based on what I see, I don't think they had a chance to set up any traps. I also think we can assume we will wait right here for you guys. Sarge looks like she will be busy for a while."

"Affirmative, cover her back, and we will be there as we clear this stairway."

Scanlon nodded at his two men and ducked under the floating blue dots.

His partners slid low, and after checking out the room, they cleared the next set of steps and started downward.

"Thomlinson, I want you to mark that door in such a way that we can't miss it. Then I want you to go in and join the sergeant and Aero. They might get too complacent and something unexpected could happen. Don't let them go any deeper, even if you have to tie up the sergeant. That is an order."

"Affirmative, Boss."

Thomlinson turned and nodded at Teve. "Okay, big guy, we go under the wire and through the door and down the yellow brick road."

Teve ducked down and easily moved. "I did not see a yellow brick road."

Thomlinson smiled. "Don't worry, it's nonsense from an old story. Let's go join the sergeant, and you can keep her from going anywhere else as ordered. There is no way I can hold her long enough to tie her up."

Ducking under the wire, Thomlinson approached the square panel with holes. He looked over at Teve. "We enter as fast as possible when this door opens."

Teve nodded, still managing to look fierce in a toga.

One downward swipe, and the door opened. They both walked into the dim blue-lit hallway. It was only a short walk to get to the double doors, and Thomlinson took a quick look, then pushed through.

Aero smiled and waved from where he was positioned near some equipment covered in dust. Sarge was speaking into her notepad and ignored them completely.

Mags looked at her first new alien find. Her estimate was that it had lain there until it just dried out. There was damage to the back of the skull, because under the dust there was an indent that was jagged.

Without looking away from the skeleton, she spoke over her shoulder. "Aero, I need help to get its clothes off without disturbing the body."

Someone handed her a vibrating knife and kneeled beside her. "Good. Now, as I cut the legs of the pants, just lay them open so I can see the skeleton underneath. Don't disturb anything as I take shots to keep a record."

Mags made a clean cut up the back of the pant leg, throwing up dust as the vibrating knife sliced with ease through the strange material.

As she leaned back, she was aware that the hands pulling the material apart belonged to Teve. She took a breath, fought to forget about one alien kneeling beside her as she examined the body of another.

Using her hand-held pad, she took a measurement of the thighbone. "Sixty centimeters. This breed is as tall as yours, Teve."

"Only the warrior sects are tall. You should study us like you are studying this breed, Sergeant." Teve's whisper was not coming through her implant, so the others would not hear his comment in their earbuds.

She shook her head to dispel his words and returned to her notes but couldn't help using him to point out her thoughts.

"There were no bugs here to eat on the flesh, and the air holds little moisture. He dried up, almost like a mummy. If his brain was in his skull like ours, the damage to the skull killed him. He was struck from behind."

Taking more pictures, she put on protective gloves and felt

the dried skin and tendons wrapped around the bones. "The bones are still whole and strong. It would take strength or a bone saw to alter them now."

"This being was strong and would seem to have been healthy when taken down. It doesn't seem to have a weapon on it or near it, as there is nothing else that I can see within the light coating of dust. Whatever killed it moved on and left it to dry up at this location."

Scanlon heard Aero in his earbud. "Hey, Thomlinson. What do you think these gadgets might be?"

"This looks like a console with a soft covering of dust. Aero, help me get rid of the dust, but don't touch anything. Just blow everything clean."

Scanlon was listening to his team as they were working their way down the steps. There was no fast way down now that they were aware of the invisible wires, so all it took was a process of throwing out a cleaning net and waiting for all strands to settle.

Scanlon asked the important question. "How many nets do we have left? I have twelve, as I didn't use any."

Tumbler reported in with nine and Ski said he had six left.

"Okay guys, let's hope this stairway is only a few floors and not fifty." Scanlon flashed his light around as they reached a turnaround to start on down to another group that should lead to a room opening. It might also have the invisible wire, so careful movement was still required.

In the meantime, he listened to Thomlinson and Aero trying to get dust from something without touching it. He then heard the sarge speak through her implant. The woman was great with ideas. It probably was one of the reasons the Colonel had attached her to their group.

Mags stopped what she was doing and looked over at the two men who were blowing at dust and coughing. "Hey, guys, unload one of your weapons and then shoot it with a full blast at the item. The inside blast will send enough pressure to push the air and clean off whatever you are looking at."

The two marines looked at each other for a moment with eyebrows raised.

Thomlinson won the silent debate. Aero turned with weapon ready to cover everyone's back and Thomlinson stripped down his own weapon and put it on full load. He aimed it right above the console and pulled the trigger.

He expected to only hear the trigger click but was happy and surprised when a wide swath of dust was immediately cleared from the face of the chest-high console. Five more clicks and a couple of small puffs from his own mouth allowed him to look over what he decided was a working station.

Exactly what the working station controlled was a question he couldn't answer — yet.

"Hey, I have uncovered a working station. It controls something, and I could turn it on."

Scanlon's voice was bumpy as he was hurrying down the cleared steps. "Is it the part that controls the ship?"

"Well, Boss, if this is a ship, this isn't the control center. But we might get some answers if we turn it on." Thomlinson waited for orders.

Scanlon huffed. "You're my expert. Turn it on slowly and try not to alert anything else. I would prefer to find you guys not fighting groups of unknowns by the time we reach you."

"Aye, sir."

Tumbler had cleared four more landings for them and they had cautiously passed two more floors, one that was without lights. They were moving along pretty smoothly when they came to a section that should have been a landing for a room. The landing was full of something.

Their flashlights showed what look like big chunks of some type of soft material similar to the type used in pillows or mattresses.

"Thomlinson and Aero, we have a problem. There is a bunch of junk blocking our way. It is piled all the way to the ceiling." Scanlon spoke as he watched Tumbler and Ski pulling some of the stuff away. Their efforts just seemed to allow more to settle onto the steps.

The sergeant's voice came through the earbuds. "Teve and I were trapped on the floor with that pile of debris. We found a way of moving through them. It was to move like you were swimming in water."

That was all she said as she went back to taking samples and making notes.

The three men looked at each other and at the pile as their lights went over the multi-colored debris.

Scanlon spoke only to the two men with him. "The lady says swim, so we will swim. Swim to the top to stay away from the chance there might be one of those invisible wires, and let's see how far this mess continues down the stairwell."

They pulled on face and breathing masks, taped their big weapons to their bodies and made sure they could get to their small guns. Together they stepped into the spongy mess and tried to pull their body upward with hands and feet spread, as if swimming.

CHAPTER TWENTY-TWO

Thomlinson had the console clear, using his own breath to clean out the holes that operated everything in front of him. The problem he saw was there were so many holes and combinations that it would take too long to figure out which would operate what part of the plates in front of him.

"Sergeant, we need you over here." Thomlinson spoke in his earbud.

"I'm busy right now." she answered, still taking notes.

"Well, Sarge, ,here are a bunch of holes on this board, and you know how Aero loves to fuck with these things. I think it would be smarter if you and I figure out what they control instead."

That got her attention. She stood up and looked at Teve, who was kneeling beside the dried body.

"Don't touch anything." She didn't look at him as she gave the order. Instead, she hurried over to move beside Thomlinson to look at the clean console. The marine was correct, there were many groups of holes, and she needed to take a moment and look at everything.

"Now look at this fine instrument. What do we have here? If we were building this console to control something, what purpose would it serve?"

Teve moved up behind her and the two marines flanked her, listening to her think out loud. Aero stated to say something, but Teve put his hand out with a shake of his head. They stood and watched the scientist think and work.

"Okay, it was close to a door and not far from the wall. The wall must have been a barrier. So, I would build this to let me check on things. I could stand here and check on the integrity of the wall and see what was going on, so I would want to check on each floor beyond the wall. I would also make the items I used the most to be close by and easiest to reach."

She slowly reached out and swiped upward over the holes closest to her as she stood in the middle.

As Thomlinson watched, two flat black areas lit up and showed areas inside two of the floors. These two floors were lit up, and one showed a row of rolling robots standing silently against the wall.

There was no movement in the other room. These two screens allowed views of the area beyond the barrier wall. She tried just covering three holes, and the scenes changed. One screen was dark, and the other showed a lit, empty room.

"I think the black screen is working and showing a dark floor. The problem is, I have no idea how many floors are in this immense housing." The sergeant reached for another set of holes and then decided that they needed to be covered too, and she was too short. She reminded herself to use the tools available.

"Teve, step up here. I need your long reach."

When she moved over, Teve was beside her, standing in the middle position at the console.

Mags nodded. "Those two sets of holes outside the screens need to be swiped down at the same time. I believe they will turn on the next set of screens."

What they got were a couple of floating screens that popped up above the console. Aero was looking over their shoulders.

"Hey, Sarge, that one screen looks like the stairs. Can we find the other guys?" Aero tried to get in closer.

Teve was reaching towards the holes when the sarge pulled at his arm. "Use your hand on the screen."

Teve looked down at her for only a second and then reached up and gently put a finger on the screen and slid it down. Sure enough, the screen slowly moved down the stairs. It was not exactly the direction they wanted to go, but it showed the steps.

Taking a moment longer, he moved his finger more slowly and got the screen to move down in the direction they wanted to show the steps. The color of the screen was a strange blue. All of them knew their eyes hadn't seen anything but a lack of light when they had been in the stairwell.

"Whatever scanning device they use picks up on a difference value than what our eyes see. Like looking through the night vision goggles and seeing everything in a different spectrum."

"Like what I see in the dark," Teve said.

Stepping back, the sarge looked up at Teve. "What color spectrum do you see when you are looking into dark areas?"

"Green and orange, with mostly dark outlines."

"Look." Aero yelled. He was not trying to be quiet. There was a pile of blue debris covering the stairwell. "It's moving."

It was moving because hefty marines were remembering their training. They'd had their turns of swimming through mud, swamp grass, salty marshes and any wet places that tried to impede their need to proceed. But they found they could use the odd shaped items to push themselves forward.

They tried keeping their backs against the down sloping ceiling. It was a hard and muscle tearing job. The sergeant had told them how to stop and not move to rest. As long as they had their bodies spread out, they were just part of the junk.

Scanlon was concerned about the fact that they were all exerting themselves too hard to get past this pile. How far did they have to go?

"This is Sergeant Bloom. We have found a way to see the stairwell and the pile of debris that blocked your team. How are you doing?"

Scanlon stopped, spreading out arms and legs, feeling the ceiling against one boot heel.

"Sergeant, I am worried about our men. This is hard work trying to get through this mess."

Aero broke in. "Lieutenant , we have good news and better news. The sarge found a way for us to see the stairway. We are looking at the pile of junk, and it's not that big. We also have a view of where there are those killer wires and there are none near you guys."

Thomlinson broke in with a chuckle. "He's right. The pile wants to just tumble down the steps, but you guys can ride it with no worries for a couple of floors. We can tell you when you are getting close to the next wire, so we will just sit here and guide you down to our level."

Aero and Thomlinson talked the three guys on the stairs down a couple of floors until they came to a wire. This time, the three men just accepted the word of their two watches and lay down on the steps to slide under the danger and then continued down.

Mags returned to the large, dried body, ignoring the fact that Teve joined her. She was now going through the pockets and carefully lying out the items onto a sterile pad that could turn into a foldable box.

She needed to figure out a way to take these items with her to be studied carefully. It should tell others a great deal about this alien race.

"What was he running from, I wonder?"

Hearing Teve's whisper, she looked up to follow his eyes. He was looking down another dimly blue-lit hallway.

Mags looked at the door they had come through to enter this area. Now she looked at the position of the body. She wasn't a forensic medic, but she was a scientist through and through. This being had been heading toward somewhere when someone or something had taken away a part of his skull.

She was thinking aloud again. "Could something get past that wire?"

"We did." Teve whispered.

Her mind that loved to put puzzles together, couldn't come up with the right answer. "Something that was not smart enough to escape from the rolling robots could not figure out how to get around that wire. Also, they were big, really big. There had to be two threats to this being."

His eyes, who seemed to disappear in this light, turned to look at her instead of the body. "Are they still here?"

Looking down at the body, Mags shook her head. "I don't know. But I think something went terribly wrong. I bet we will find other bodies, maybe of different types, if we search the rest of the container. I think a terrible disaster happened and something went wrong. It took a decision that would eventually kill a lot of the beings that built this metal unit."

Teve let out a sigh. "I respect your intuition. Are there more traps in this vessel?"

Looking down the new hallway, Mags had a sad smile. "I think there are a lot of traps. For reasons we may never know, they were transporting or holding dangerous live beings on this container. Perhaps it was to study some dangerous captives, or maybe the captives were some types of enemy. I think it is too treacherous for us to study them in any detail.

I think we are going to be fighting for our lives to just get back off this container, due to the traps that have been activated. I want so badly to go down that hallway and discover what else lies ahead. But my own self-preservation says I

won't put my hand into fire, so I think we need to tell the lieutenant what I feel about this situation."

She glanced at the screen—they were making progress
with Aero and Thomlinson talking in his ear. The lieutenant,
Ski, and Tumbler had fought their way out of the soft pile of
debris and slid through the last of the pieces to go on down
the steps.

Thomlinson examined the downward direction the marines were heading, looking for danger, wires, and anything
that might impede their progress.

Mags could hear the conversations and directions behind
her as she looked at the hallway ahead. Again, she looked at
the body.

"He wasn't heading for the hallway." She closed up her ev-
idence box and sealed it to its smallest size. Standing up, she
got to the feet of the body and looked across the body at the
wall that was the start before the hallway. It was made of
metal panels with no small panel of holes to be seen anywhere.

"Hey, Sarge." Aero said behind her. "Thomlinson is guid-
ing the Boss down the stairs and it is going pretty smooth.
Unfortunately, it's going to take them a couple of hours to get
here. OK if we belly up and get some protein?"

Distracted, Mags looked around from the point where she
was standing. "Aero, where do you think this guy was heading?"

"Don't know, Sarge. Could be any direction. The blow to
his head could have sent him to that position, depending
what hit him and with how much strength."

Knowing that Aero might be right, she was still curious to
figure it out. "Take turns helping the team move down the
stairs. Eat and drink on alert." She hoped she was giving the
right commands. She wasn't used to giving orders to marines
in the field, and she was more interested in the body in front

of her.

"If I am running towards the hallway and get hit that hard in the back of the head, I would fall . . ." Thinking out loud again, Mags stared at the panels.

"On your side." It was Teve who finished the thought.

"So, where was he going?" She had now moved to the head of the body, her back to it. "Aero, can you give me one of the big flashlights?"

Aero passed a big light to Teve, who passed it to Mags, who didn't want to move from her position facing a metal wall. She used the big light at its brightest and largest coverage to illuminate several metal panels of the wall leading to the hallway.

"What do you see with your intuition?" Teve's whispered question was just for her.

"There. One panel that is just too smooth." She let the light narrow down and highlight the panel she was studying.

"It has no holes for entry." Teve's sharp eyes were also studying the panel.

"Perhaps it is a special trap. One that might be triggered in an emergency to open as a being slams against it to get away from danger?" She stepped forward, looking at the details of the panel as it fit tightly against the rest of the metal panels. All the other panels had metal studs and even some rough edges holding them in place.

This one panel was smooth and seamlessly tight up against the metal on all four sides, even the floor. With the floor covered in the dust, she couldn't see any marks. She stepped closer and kneeled to brush dust off the floor about a foot from the panel.

There were no marks on the metal floor, so if the panel opened, it went in or up or sideways. But her mind told her that just didn't seem right, either. With no holes to swipe, Mags stepped up and pounded on the metal panel to see if it sounded different from the others.

Everything happened lightning fast. She stepped up with her body almost touching the panel and her fist above her head to slam into the door. She heard Teve grunt as he moved in an accelerated way of his to stop her, and he was against her body as the panel flipped around. It spun on an axis, threw them from the area where they'd just been, and instantly closed with a sharp metal clank.

Mags still had her light, and she soon saw several things that she didn't like. First, the room was small and dark. Next, there were two dead dried bodies sitting together in one corner. Last there was the warm body of Teve that she was leaning against behind her.

On the outside of the room, Aero was standing there about to pull out some water when he saw the sarge and the big Veldan just disappear.

"Hey, Thomlinson, we have a royal SNAFU."

"Handle it, buddy. I am helping the team." Thomlinson now had the dark stairwell up on two floating screens. He had found a way of using his glove over his penlight to extend his reach and was getting used to the console.

"I think this is going to make the lieutenant really unhappy." Aero took a few steps backward to stand beside Thomlinson, facing the wall.

"Thomlinson, the wall swallowed Sarge and Teve." Aero's voice was strong enough to draw his partner's attention.

CHAPTER TWENTY-THREE

It took four and a half hours to get the other two guys down the stairs and into the hallway. They came immediately to the area with the alien dead body and the console that Thomlinson was working.

Ski suddenly pumped his arm in the air. "I have contact with the skip ship."

"Good. Report our location with as much detail as you can give them. Give them the news about Deeks. See if you can send any type of bouncing signal that will help them find us. That might help us find how to get out of here."

He looked around the dusty area and saw the flash set up that had the body and the wall beyond in white light.

"Someone tell me everything about our lab rat?" His voice let everyone around him know it wasn't a request.

Ski and Tumbler took over the console equipment. This allowed the two marines in trouble to move up beside the lieutenant and try to decide who should speak first.

Aero realized he knew the most, so it was up to him to do the talking. He explained how they'd been more concerned with getting the team down through the stair. It seemed to him and Thomlinson that the four in this room were safe and that the priority was getting the rest down the stairs and getting everyone together.

He explained that the sarge was in her scientist mode. She was really interested in the body and discovering anything she could about that dried up body.

"She started talking about how it didn't look like the alien was trying to go down the hallway. Tumbler called me over when you guys passed those two dark floors.

I heard her say something about panels, and whatever Teve said, I couldn't understand. They weren't talking with earbuds. She asked for a big light, and I passed one to Teve, who handed it to her.

The next thing I heard, while watching the screens for you guys, was a type of thump, like a fist hitting the wall and then a metal clank. When I turned around, I couldn't see Teve or the sarge."

Aero pointed at the light. "When I took another large light, I could see where their footprints in the dust ended up in that swirl at the wall. I checked it and pushed it and even Thomlinson tried it. We just waited for you guys before trying anything drastic."

Inside the box, both Mags and Teve were exhausted. They had attempted every trick they could think of to get the door to open. They then turned to the walls of the six-foot by eight-foot box and tried each panel to see if it would move or come loose.

Mags had reluctantly agreed to stand on Teve's broad shoulders to exert pressure against the ceiling panels. She discovered long small openings along the top of a couple of panels that let in air. She could feel the air move past her fingers when she moistened her fingers on her tongue.

When they got down on their knees to examine the floor, they found matching air ducts, less than a quarter of an inch, at the bottom of a couple panels. So they wouldn't be suffocating. That also explained the fact that there was no dust on the floor.

At Teve's insistence, they took a break and ate and drank some of the water with all the minerals from the soft bottles.

She needed to relieve her body, so she turned the light off and made Teve move over and face away.

After she sealed the disposal bag, she realized how childish her actions were concerning making him turn his back. He knew what she was doing and, as a scientist, she knew anything concerning the body was just natural. There also was a smell in the small room from her body waste. Damn, she was a complete idiot, acting like a teenage virgin.

"Teve, thank you for your consideration. I am still getting used to being in the field." She packaged some items and put what some would call trash in a corner by the panel that had swung them into the room.

Teve turned and looked at her. With the flashlight on in the small room, she could see the color of his eyes, like the ferns in the forest of her dad's farm. Not that she'd stayed there very much.

"I am afraid that I must take care of the same bodily problem, Sergeant. You may turn your back if you wish."

Mags wasn't sure what her feelings were, but she decided now would be a good time to examine the two dead bodies in the corner. She and Teve had been careful in their exploration of the small room not to disturb the dead in the one corner. Now seemed like the time to see about that situation.

She tried going through the obvious pockets while not disturbing anything. Everything was empty. Sitting back on her heels, she was puzzled. These were intelligent beings who had come from an area that had that fancy console.

She looked around as Teve came up behind her. "Does your intuition tell you why these two would lock themselves in a room like this?"

Shaking her head, she answered. "On old Earth we called these *Panic Rooms*. It actually was supposed to be a safe place that you went when you needed to get away from attackers that you might be defenseless against."

Kneeling down on one heel, he put one hand on his other raised knee and looked at the dried bodies. "They have been here a very long time. Why didn't they leave?"

"Because the threat was still out there and the door wouldn't open." Mags pointed at their clothes. "Tell me something, Teve. When you are hiking through the jungles of Veld and dressed in the clothes that would be natural for you, would you carry items in your pockets?"

He turned his head to look at her. "We wear minimum clothing in our jungles, but yes, we carry small things besides our weapons."

Nodding at the two bodies, she frowned. "So far, I have found nothing in any of their pockets that I can reach. When I work in my lab, I have all types of small items tucked into pockets. Sometimes it gets out of hand and people stop me to unload items they need.

"Even if these beings are extremely neat, I saw some small items on the console once the dust was cleared. There were lots of items on the body outside this panic area."

"So, these two might have come from a different area?" Teve asked as he looked at the bodies.

"Maybe."

"Why didn't the door open when the threat was over?" Teve now looked at Mags with that question.

Standing up, Mags had to clear her voice. "You know the answer."

He nodded. "Because the threat isn't over."

Mags tried her implant again. There wasn't even any static. The heavy walls of the room prevented any contact with the marines on the outside, and there was no way to warn them.

Teve pointed at the two bodies. "Do you want to move them?"

Nodding, Mags answered. "It is the one place we haven't tried to take apart."

The moving took a while, as the bodies tended to fall apart. Mags decided the alien beings had been in here longer than she first estimated.

Once the move was completed, the corner looked exactly like the other three in the room. Neat, seamless, well-fitting walls that had made a snug connection. There was nothing falling out of the clothes of the aliens besides a couple of additional bones that belonged to their bodies.

"Sergeant, there is something else to try."

Turning, Mags sat down in the corner and looked at the spread legs of Teve. She tried to think of anything that they hadn't tried but came up blank.

She heard his whispery voice. "In my modified form, I am extremely strong, stronger than I am now. Perhaps I could punch through a panel or the door. You must decide where would be the weakest for me, and I will change and attack it."

There were several things in her life that she didn't want to do. She didn't want to try sushi, the thought of raw fish made her skin crawl. She never wanted to go spelunking, as the idea of being on hands and knees deep in the earth with bugs and water and the thought of cave-ins was not appealing. Being trapped in a small metal box with a shifted beast just about topped her list of *not to dos*.

To take her mind off that picture, she looked around to decide what might really be the weak spot in this room. She looked up at the ceiling, close to where the air was coming in at a vent.

Teve watched her light blue eyes look up at the edge of the ceiling. Before he turned, he thought of the little bell-shaped flowers that grew near the waterfalls at the edge of the rock drops. It was not a color that was seen often on Veld, as even the sky had a lot of clouds and the trees were heavy over the land. The atmosphere was a different color, both from the dust from the desert half of his world and from the color of his sun.

She was so different from the other humans that he had come in contact with, and he knew she had mixed emotions about him. He felt her fear and anger as she tried to fight everything she felt. She was a strange female.

He finally turned and looked up to the fine sliver where the air came into the room. Perhaps she was correct. The ceiling would not need to be as fortified as the walls, or even the floor. That area where the tiny gap was built to allow air to come in might just be the one spot that his strength could break.

He could jump now and touch it, but in his modified form, he could break into the slits with his claws. He could also use his strength to slam against the ceiling at that point to see if it might be weaker.

For hours, the team had been working, trying to understand why the panel would swallow two of their people. Scanlon assigned Ski and Thomlinson to the console, searching for any threats with the floating screens. They changed the screens from one site to another. The one thing that became clear was that the inside of the container was huge and broken up into a maze.

Ski also periodically talked to the skip ship, bringing them up to date with the progress of the team. Both the skip ship and the larger grabber ship had no luck in pinpointing the team or anything else within the shell.

Scanlon and Tumbler spent the time trying to break into the panel that Aero said had taken the sarge and Teve.

They had pried off a couple of panels on the side of what seemed to be a solid metal area on both sides of the panel that had left a half circle in the dust.

Tumbler thumped on the thick wall. "We don't even know if they are in there. It could be another set of stairs. It could also be an elevator or even just a floor that drops out like we have experienced. They could be anywhere by now."

Scanlon turned to look at the backs of the two men working at the console. By this time, they had figured out how to use most of the holes.

"They didn't see any movement so far. If someone is alive on this ship, they should be able to spot it before long. But we still have to believe that two of our people are behind this swinging door." Scanlon had anger in his voice, but he kept the tone low.

"Well, any drills we tried didn't even leave a scratch. We might try a compressed explosive," Tumbler said as he was digging through one of his bags.

"If they are still in there, we have no way to warn them. The door might fly right in on them." Scanlon watched in amazement at the items Tumbler pulled from his satchel.

"Well, they've been in there ten hours. They have enough food and water for a couple of days. Maybe we should rest up, and if our tech experts don't find anything in about eight hours, we can attach the compression explosive." Thomlinson held up a black object about the size of his hand.

Scanlon liked that idea, but before he said anything, Ski called them over to the console.

Thomlinson was working on one screen, trying to follow something that was moving. The problem was that the room had almost no lights and there were a lot of shadows from piles of boxes or equipment. It was hard to identify the piles, but it was obvious something was moving through the piles.

Thomlinson pointed with a finger. "This one is in trouble, here comes one of the rolling shooters."

Even in the dim light and on the small screen, they could

recognize the small aggressive box. Except the action was strange. They watched as the blurry large figure moved from shadow to shadow and then it charged, ignoring the bullets coming from the box.

It was hard to see in the dim lighting, but it was obvious the big bi-pedal had the box up off the ground and when it was done, it threw the box away. The box was not rolling or shooting.

Aero let out the first words. "Wow, that looks like the work of Teve after he modifies and takes on the Trios. That is one impressive shadow out there."

"No, that is something pretty dangerous." Thomlinson was trying to get the camera to follow the shadow and keep it on the screen. This was all guesswork as he handled the alien console.

As fast as they found the moving shadow, they lost the whole scene as the screen jumped to another level.

Scanlon heard a couple of groans, but he just let his men do their jobs, as the two marines at the console worked to get the correct picture back. He asked for something different.

"Any chance we can see our area?"

Thomlinson needed a break, so he turned around to give an answer. "First of all, we don't know what or where the cameras might be stored. This is all alien technology and we are just guessing.

None of us could recognize anything that looked like a camera in the stairway, yet we couldn't see you guys as you moved. We accidentally found one screen on which we discovered a way to move and follow you down. It's that third screen over there that still shoots steps.

What Ski is doing now is just hunting through all the things to see if we can find one that might show this area. We're not sure how to pick and choose. All we can do is hunt and peck."

Scanlon nodded. "Okay, we have all been on our feet for

too long. I want to set up a four-hour on and four-hour down. Thomlinson, you and Ski take turns and also get the same type of rest. We need to take an eight-hour rest period, then we will get real serious about getting to Sarge and Teve and getting the hell off this ship."

Most non-combatants wouldn't understand the fact that trained men in the field could actually get rest and sleep in a stress filled situation. A smart and experienced warrior could instruct his body to take rest and food when the opportunity was presented.

After eight hours, there were five marines who considered themselves back in top shape. Scanlon told them to eat breakfast and take a piss, then go back to work.

This meant that Thomlinson and Ski worked together at the console. This let Scanlon and Tumbler attack the door that possibly held the other two people of their team.

Tumbler worked on the compression explosive. With his ability to pick off a target farther away than any other marine Scanlon had ever worked with, Tumbler also handled explosives like a pro bank robber. It took him twenty minutes to decide and place the bomb.

He taped some reflective material over the whole area to catch any blow back and held the trigger in his hand.

He warned the men at the console and he and Scanlon stepped down the hallway. He counted down and blew the explosive.

It made a nice noise and a lot of smoke and did nothing to the panel.

CHAPTER TWENTY-FOUR

Sitting on the floor and holding the beast's head in her lap, Mags heard a loud thump against the front of the box they were in, and the floor trembled slightly. Other than that, everything was still and quiet with Teve breathing as he lay on his back on the metal floor.

She had thought that nothing could hurt the shifted beast, but this time he had hurt himself. Nothing he did would put a dent in the metal room, even at the air vents. In frustration, he jumped again and again. He slammed that great body against that one point at the ceiling corner, hoping to break something loose. On one jump, he hit the corner in the wrong way, jamming his head into the corner and he just dropped.

Waiting a moment, Mags finally moved over to where the great form was lying on the metal floor, curled up on itself. It took some effort to get him onto his back. The head wound was bleeding just above a hairy eyebrow.

Hunting out a med bag, she shifted the light to give her a view of the injury. His head kept rolling away, so she finally sat down with her back against a wall and legs straight out into the room. Mags then pulled his head into her lap and cleaned the wound and sprayed sealing skin over the area.

Not knowing what else to do, she just sat with him in her lap. After a while, she moved enough to pull out some water and took a small drink, wondering if they should start rationing their intake. She pulled a sterile pad from the med pack and moistened it, then dropped a little onto the lips between the hair on his lower face.

She was surprised that the hair on his head was so long and wild, but the facial hair seemed to be short and almost trimmed in some manner. The scientist mode kicked in and she wanted to get some of his cells into her lab back on Earth.

There was movement and she looked down into those blue-green eyes underneath the heavy brows that slanted downward to give an evil look, even when he wasn't staring.

"Teve, you hit your head pretty bad. I wonder if you could change back into your other form now?"

He moved, and she slid back to allow him room. Her hand hit the blanket that he had converted into a toga and she decided he would need it if he shifted. She stood up and turned back to him, and he already was in his man form.

With the light on him, she got a full view of a large naked male. She quickly reached out the blanket and turned her eyes slowly away. She had to admit that even with a bruise on his forehead, he was quite a specimen.

Teve took the blanket, but just held it as he spoke. "Sergeant, are you a female who has not known a man, or do you prefer your own sex?"

"Are you asking me this because I'm not looking at you naked like I'm a voyeur?" She waved a hand.

"No, because you are always interested, in me and yet you fight it, like a *bensail* in a hole."

She stepped forward in anger. "What the hell is a *bensail*?"

She saw his smile for the first time. "A small jungle cat that has a temper too big for its size."

"I don't have a temper." She took a deep breath. It was at that point that she realized she was face to face with a really tall naked man who was holding a blanket. Worse, she had yelled right in his face.

She searched her mind for an answer for her actions and wondered what she should do next. This was so different for her — she was now left speechless.

She finally stepped back. "I'm sorry I was yelling. I think it is the stress."

She put her hand out on his chest and was surprised at the warmth. She should have removed her hand immediately, but she stopped and looked at her pale hand on his darker skin. There were no sounds in the room except for their breathing. Hers was shorter and his was long and deeper.

Then, as if mesmerized, she saw him place his hand over hers and slowly move up her uniform covered arm until he reached her shoulder. Even with the uniform protecting her, she imagined she felt the heat of that hand.

She stood in this solid, inescapable room with this man from another world that was not Earth, and they were going to die here, just like the two beings bunched up in the corner.

With a kick of her foot, she knocked over the light, turning it off and leaving them in the darkness. Then, for the first time since leaving the skip ship, she turned and removed the MA12 without the backup cover of a teammate.

Thinking how stupid it was to be in the dark with someone who could see in the dark, she placed the weapon against the wall and began taking off her clothes to stack next to the weapon in a pile. It seemed that as she took off all the marine apparel, she disconnected her mind from the restrictions of what had held her together for years.

"I have known a couple of men, not had a long-term commitment. But I prefer men to women. I know we are probably going to die in here, and I don't know why I harbored the feelings against shape shifters. It seems I have to face the fact that I am actually fascinated by you. Now seems like the time for me to face my own feelings."

Suddenly he lifted her up and enclosed her in his arms, and she welcomed the warmth of his large body. Without hesitation, she wrapped her arms around his neck and let her weight hang from the broad shoulders.

"Thank you." Teve whispered in her ear.

Her giggle surprised her. "After all I said and did, you only whisper a couple of words?"

Through his chest, she heard the words even better. "They were the right words." He whispered.

Without thought, she found her legs twisting around his waist and she had only a moment to wonder why this all felt like the right thing she should be doing.

Even in the blackness of this room, she was there at his face, feeling his breath. She reached with her tongue and tasted his cheek.

"I will not be able to stop if you continue that stroke." He pulled her tighter.

Oh, it was a challenge she could not refuse. She used her tongue to find that cheek again and then slid down the jaw. Mags finished by tasting that full bottom lip, but before she could draw away, he sucked her tongue in and she felt his teeth.

A thrill caused a shiver down her back from the points of those alien teeth that still were gentle and let her reclaim her tongue. His tongue followed hers to taste and assert some demands of his own. Her teasing had a price. She was the Grand Prize winner.

He turned, and with her hands behind his neck, she felt the cold wall. He was leaning against it and shielding her body. She had this large warm heating blanket between her almost naked body and the cold metal wall. She scooted her feet down against his wide body and remained spread across him, enjoying the feel of male muscles between her legs.

She tilted her head back as he gently raked those pointed teeth against her exposed neck. She knew he could destroy an enemy in one bite, but the feeling she had of his control and the trust she placed in him brought moisture to an important female place.

Teve's whisper stirred her hair. "I smell you."

She was glad she couldn't see him and wished he couldn't see her. "I haven't had a shower in days." Her voice had an apology in it, but she wasn't going to back off.

The chest echoed his chuckle. "I smell your heat and female need. It is such a sweet smell."

His strength was so great that she had to close her eyes to what he did next. He had his hands gripping her under her arms and was lifting her up, higher and higher, until she slipped away, leaving go of him. She reached out and placed her palms against the cold wall as she felt his hot face move down her body while he held her over his head.

At last, his mouth found her mound, and she sucked in a breath. She knew when she let it out, it came with the small scream as his tongue worked her clit. Without thought, she had a knee on his shoulder and he had his mouth working that female area that had almost never been touched.

It took his tongue and a soft scrape of those sharp teeth to bring her to her first orgasm, and that was when the scream and breath let go along with her body.

He lowered her slowly, down his front and within the heat of his wide shoulders, over the deep chest, and then there was the prod of the male member waiting for entrance to her realm that was now wet and ready.

With her knees still up, he glided her down on the male organ that waited for her. He had made her more than ready as her body enclosed him. Even though it had been a long time since she had enjoyed sex and she was tight and small, his large male distention insisted on entrance.

There was only a first second of discomfort for her, and then it was bliss. He was filling her and hitting every spot inside of her that demanded attention, over and over.

This time, after several of the strong movements of his body into hers, they reached that special place together. He let go with an animal sound and she just tore her sore throat.

He let the wall hold them as he moved down to collapse and hold her curled up in his lap. They both were covered with the smell of sex and some fluids.

Through the next hours, with and without the light, they shared in the act again, both getting a feeling of more than just satisfaction. Something was building between the two people from different worlds.

There was very little conversation, but a lot of comfort for these two who believed they were going to die in this room in another few hours.

CHAPTER TWENTY-FIVE

The crew had given up on trying to get the strange swinging door open. There were more important things to take care of, like whatever that big thing was that tore apart shooting boxes.

Another sixteen-hour day had gone by, and Scanlon was giving orders for night rest for the team. They had to do something soon, as personal supplies were running low.

He made sure everyone took the vitamin supplements in the med packs and insisted that water intake be normal. They could live longer without food, but the body needed water.

Aero was working on the console screens and suddenly called Thomlinson over. Thomlinson was just about to settle down for the first four-hour break. He shrugged and joined his partner at the alien workstation.

They talked quietly and then agreed on something.

Aero turned to speak to the lieutenant. "Boss, I think we have found a way out, and it is close to our location."

Scanlon listened as the two marines worked out the target of exit that they had found on the screens. At the end of the hallway was a large vent that seemed to belong to what would be called an engineering section on an Earth ship.

"If we can get into this section with the machinery, there is an airlock right here." Thomlinson pointed at a screen that showed what looked like a schematic of a part of the container or ship or whatever it might turn out to be.

Aero added a comment. "It looks like it might get a little cramped in the vents as they turn right here . . ." he pointed at a screen, "but once we get past that tight spot, it seems the tunnel is bigger. We are going to have to instruct the skip ship to come around to this side of the ship to pick us up. We don't have our off-ship suits, so they will have to attach somehow to get us into the skip ship. But they have done that before, so it is all possible."

Scanlon stood looking at the path they would have to take. What was taking him a while to make up his mind was that he still had two live team members missing.

He looked at Tumbler. "Sharpshooter, are we going to get that door open on our own?"

Tumbler shook his head. "I am out of ideas. My guess is that it was built to be impregnable. If our two people are in there, we will need something better than what I have available."

Scanlon kneeled down on one heel. "Okay, guys, listen up. We are going to have one hour. We are going to repack and make sure everything is secure. Aero, I want you to leave some type of message in case Teve and the sarge get out of that door. We need to tell them where we went.

Thomlinson, find some way to copy that schematic so we don't get lost, and if we have to make a detour, find us some place to go that still leads to that equipment room."

Within two hours, five fully armed men were butt-crawling through a vent that they had pried open at the wall. The wall was only two turns down the blue-lit hallway before they found the large outlet. It was high in the tall hallway, but a little cooperation between backs and shoulders soon got the men all up and on their knees. Butt crawling meant the first guy had a view and the last guy crawled backwards. The rest looked at the ass of the guy ahead. Butt crawling.

The marines were surprised at how quiet it was in the round vent and how they could move through the curved pipe without making noise. Just like the rooms and walls outside the stairwell, the pipe was lined with something that was the same pale sand color.

Aero had written a long note on the floor outside the strange door to tell the two missing teammates where the rest of them had gone. There were also arrows and a drawing of the schematic in case the screen closed down at the console. He left another large flashlight and water and protein bars for them, just in case they might have run short of their own supplies.

He ended with a big *follow the yellow brick road*. He thought about Sarge making the wisecrack when he had asked how he could get one of the MA12s. She had made a reference to *click your heels*, and he remembered it was from an old Earth story. After those big words, he added the long arrow showing the direction that the team was heading down the hall.

Two hours of crawling was tiring, so Scanlon ordered a short rest. They spread out and lay down, mostly to relieve their bent knees. It was good that they had time for the break, as the next vent they needed to go through was the smaller one that required that they snake through on their bellies.

Pushing weapons ahead and everything else on their backs, they actually made good time through the clean pipe. No one spoke, not even in the earbuds, concerned about what rooms might be around the pipe.

Back on their stomachs, the team moved smoothly. Tumbler was in front with his special weapon and gave a double click when he reached the point where they needed to turn into the larger vent.

Aero took the time to draw arrows for the two that were missing, and they all moved forward carefully. This was the largest vent, and it seemed more like what they expected in air vents. It was square and seemed to be made from lightweight metal. The marines took no chances and spread out to keep their own weight distributed along the channel.

"Hey, Boss, we need to stop at this point." Aero and Thomlinson had a drawing out and the wind in the square tunnel was pushing at their clothes.

Thomlinson pointed. "If we go much further, we are going to run into the machines that circulate the air. We need to break through this vent and drop into the equipment room."

Understanding what was needed, Scanlon nodded and took up the back position as guard. Tumbler could move to help to open up a thin piece of the bottom of the vent to allow them to drop in. The decision was to do as little damage as possible and try to repair it so that they did not draw attention to the fact that they were intruders on the ship.

They got a clean cut and pulled the piece to one side. Tumbler set up what was left of his piece of climbing rope and they began sliding down to the room below.

Aero wrote some instructions next to the metal piece and left the second piece of climbing rope that Scanlon had, so that the other two could get down to the floor below if they made it this far in the pipes.

Tumbler was last man out. Hanging by a hand to a piece of something on the outside of the vent, he worked the cut piece of metal back into position and sprayed a coating of rubber along the edges. He finally looked down to see the area clear below in the well-lit, cluttered room.

He took a deep breath and dropped, tucking his legs before he hit the floor to roll. The jolt still knocked the air from his lungs and he felt the pull on one shoulder, but he was fine as the guys helped him stand.

Ski was in contact with the skip ship that moved around the unknown large metal oval to find the exit lock that was in this room.

"Okay, we need to go to the outside wall and then find that exit point." Scanlon nodded, and they began to move among the big alien machinery.

"This place is pretty big with a lot of really huge machines, but it seems awful quiet. Are they running, or shut down?" Ski asked as he looked at a large, convoluted item that loomed over him with protrusions that stuck out in all directions.

Thomlinson answered in his earbud. "Something is moving the air, and on this ship, something is creating the air or taking it from storage tanks. This is really some high-tech stuff. Not all working machinery needs to make a noise."

At that point, everyone froze in ready position at the sound of something crashing in the distance.

"Aero, is that the direction we need to go to find that port exit?" Scanlon asked in the earbud.

"I'm afraid so. Maybe it was just a box that fell over." Just as Aero spoke, there was another rumble that sounded like a bunch of boxes had fallen.

"Fuck." No one admitted to the utterance as they grouped together.

Scanlon looked around. "First item is to find the outer wall. Aero, Thomlinson, do you remember anything from what you saw on the screens?"

The two marines looked up at the large vent they had vacated and then around where they all stood.

"Over that way. They would have put this stuff away from the outer walls, so once we get past this big stuff, we will find small stuff that they probably just stored in a useless space." Thomlinson spoke as he worked his way past the big equipment.

This piece of machinery was the size of the skip ship. As they made their way carefully around it, they found their way blocked by something just as large. It was like making their way through a maze.

As they started their slow plod around the next equipment, they heard the slamming and banging of something in the remoteness of the large irregular room they were exploring.

Chapter Twenty-Six

Sometimes with the light on, but mostly with the light off, Mags and Teve made love or slept or just held on to each other. Teve put his long body stretched out on the floor and let Mags keep warm on top of him.

She didn't get much sleep as she thought about the situation. She thought of the irony. Mags had never felt so close to a man in her life, and it turned out to be at a point when she probably was going to die. To make it even more interesting, she had gotten over her fear of shape shifters. Her bias against the people of the planet U231Z42—or Veld—had all disappeared as she heard the heartbeat of the one she lay against.

She moved as cool air hit her naked back. "You tore my undershirt off."

"I cut it off, remember my special nails?" He chuckled. "I need a drink. Do we ration the water, or just take what we need now?"

Laughing, Mags rolled off him. She rolled sideways, and her arm hit the door. It slid open, standing sideways in the circle it created.

"Oh, my God. Teve quick, stop it from closing." She got to her feet but knew he would be faster. She was right, as he was up and in the opening with his bare ass against the half-open door.

Looking around at her clothes, she grabbed some to hold in front of her. "Can you hold it while I get dressed, or do I need to toss everything out?"

Leaning his tall body, without letting go of the door, he

looked around. "Sergeant, there is no one here. The team is gone."

"Oh. Okay, let me toss everything out and get settled out there." With those words, Mags began tossing things past Teve's long legs. She picked up the light and looked around to see what she'd missed.

There were a couple of small items and Teve's toga blanket. With these and the light, she then squeezed past the large man and was outside the room she'd thought she was destined to die within.

Teve let go of the door, and as he stepped away, it slammed shut with a clang. It was the same sound that they'd heard when they'd first been swept into the rooms.

Mags took only a moment to look around, seeing some screens still floating above the console. She decided it was time to get dressed. She took her torn undershirt and wiped down her body, smelling sex and Teve on her skin. Finally, discarding that rag, she got dressed as a marine in most of the layers that she had been outfitted in when they started their journey.

Ending with the backpack over her shoulders and her special MA12 hanging in front, she was ready. The note from her departed team was obviously on the floor, but first she wanted to look at the console.

There was one screen that was strange, and she knew that Thomlinson and Aero had left it active for a purpose. She stared up at it for a moment and then saw movement within the shadows and dim lights.

"Teve, there is someone else in this container."

"The team?" Teve asked as he finished his toga.

"No, something big that is hiding."

"So, what do you want to do? Do we go look at that big shadow, or do we follow the signs left by the team?"

She turned around and looked at the big man in a toga and

realized he was serious. He would take whichever route she chose and would not try to influence her in whatever her choice. He would have her back and protect her and let her lead.

This was something that she had never experienced before and it gave her a strange feeling inside. How could she separate herself from this male from a different planet when the project was completed?

"We do the smart thing and try to join our team. They had some reason for going in this direction." Mags tried her implant but got no response.

"Come on Teve. I am not sure how far behind them we are, but we can't stand around. Let's see where the arrows lead us."

"Are you going to let me lead?" Teve was looking at the words and arrows.

"I have the weapon that will kill faster than anything. You should protect my back. If it gets bad, you must change. I'm sorry, do your modify thing and save us both." She nodded and took a position next to the wall of the hall.

There was enough blue light to give a decent view down the length of it until there was a turn in the hallway. She knew they were behind, but now was not the time to get careless. Especially after she'd seen that shadow move in the room on the screen. There was something else inside the unit.

"Teve, what do you think they were hauling in this thing?" Mags kept her voice low, but she knew Teve could hear a faint whisper. When he did his first change to protect her as they fell from one floor to another with the pile of debris, he'd lost his earbud.

She had learned that both in this form and in his altered form, his hearing was better than human. She thought about other talents he had and smiled as heat spread through her body.

"Female, I smell you, and if you do not think of other things, I will insist we stop to take care of certain needs. It will make a long trip."

Mags shook her head and adjusted her weapon. She was almost at the junction and wasn't stopping now, not even for the thoughts that were going through her mind. She got down low, remembering at what height the rolling shooters sprayed bullets.

She wondered why she hadn't brought her makeup kit. She had a nice small mirror tucked inside, but makeup kits were not on the marine field kit list. Without the mirror, she did a quick peek and, finding the hallway clear, took a long look to ensure she missed nothing. Standing up, she felt Teve's warm hand on her back. She glanced over her should and he was facing the other way, just checking on her location.

Still in the low whisper, she spoke. "Hallway is clear and I see additional arrows from the team."

In this slow, nerve-wracking method and after two turns, the two people made their way to the last area that showed arrows and an open-air vent above their heads.

It had taken them hours just to reach this spot, and although Teve showed no fatigue, Mags was feeling the toll on her body. Teve looked down and her. She smiled as she read a note on the wall that had to be from the marine who read the same old books she did. It read *FOLLOW THE YELLOW BRICK ROAD*. It was followed by an arrow that pointed to the air vent above.

"Take a break and I will watch. Get some water and a protein bar and then you will be ready to get up into that air vent. I will have the pleasure of watching you crawl ahead of me."

She smiled and shook her head at the thoughts his words brought to mind. She also knew he was right. She let him do his thing as she sat down with her back to the wall, her MA12 across her chest. She got water out to wash down the food bar and even dug out some vitamins from the med pack.

She allowed herself about a half hour and decided she would either go to sleep for eight hours or get up now and start on the next leg of this *follow the arrows* journey.

Getting into the vent was easy with Teve's height and strength. As for him, he jumped once and got half his body into the opening and soon pulled his legs in behind him.

Now they had to crawl, with Mags leading and Teve taking up a lot of room behind her.

"Sergeant, can you reach the team through your earbud?"

Touching behind her ear, she spoke but got nothing, not even static. "No, I think it is the coating on this pipe. It is like the same color as the rooms that we traveled through. I think it is made on purpose to interfere with communication devices or maybe certain weapons."

"Yet your weapon works."

"We have no idea what type of weapons the beings that own this strange tube might use. We also don't know what type of weapons their enemies might use against them, if they have enemies."

Moving on knees and hands became tiring, and Mags thought Teve was talking to distract her.

"Are you trying to keep my mind busy on something but the pain in my knees?"

She heard a chuckle.

"I am trying to keep my mind off the curves on the ass that is moving so close in front of me. It is hard crawling with a fifth limb."

That took her mind off her knees as she pictured the short blanket wrapped around a large male body. She wondered how long this section of the pipe was going and if she could make it any faster.

After an hour, she had no choice but to take a break. They both lay down on their backs and stretched out legs. It was harder to relax the shoulders, but raising the arms above her head and pushing brought some relief.

Mags looked at her arm timer and decided they could only rest for ten minutes. She was sure the trained marines would have made better time through this tube.

CHAPTER TWENTY-SEVEN

After following a maze of large quiet machinery, the five finally found what Thomlinson declared was the outer wall.

"This looks like a pretty solid metal wall. How do you know we are in the right place?" Scanlon spoke as he put one hand on the wall in question.

Everyone jumped at the crashing sounds that seemed to be coming closer. Tumbler and Aero were on point and alert, weapons pointing out as they looked around the equipment.

"Look up. Eventually, you are going to see that the wall is gently dropping in over our heads. It isn't much, because this is such a large ship or container."

Craning his neck up, he saw the wall slanting over them in the high room with numerous levels of bare screen walkways and floating lights. Thomlinson was correct in that the wall was not straight.

They were standing between piles of odd-shaped items, all smaller than the big machinery and piled on top of each other. The piles were higher than they could reach, maybe twenty feet high.

Scanlon looked around. "So, what the hell is all of this stuff? It's going to make it tough following the wall to find the exit door."

"Hey." Aero spoke through his earbud. "Where do we throw our extra stuff? The stuff we want out of the way when we are on the skip ship?"

Scanlon smiled as he remembered everyone throwing totes

against the walls, out of the way to keep the aisle clear. This was the final storage area for the least used small items for the beings that built or used this craft. It was a treasure trove that he knew his people would love to take years to go through and see what they could discover.

He could foresee two problems. The first one was that they would always have to move away from the wall to go around these piles. The second one was worse, as a pile could be in front of that exit port.

Right now, he had a big problem to solve, and it was to find out what was causing all the noise. Aero and Thomlinson had told him the hard facts. The direction they needed to go was towards whatever was causing the noise.

Looking around, he saw what was called catwalks in English. There were numerous screen and wire types, hanging walkways in various stages above the machinery and the air vent they had used to enter this area.

"Thomlinson, find a way to get up on one of those walkways and be our eyes."

The marine nodded and hooked his weapon over his shoulder. He was a rock climber extraordinaire. Scampering up the side of odd-shaped equipment, he found hand and footholds that they hadn't seen from the floor.

Tumbler took the place beside Aero to stand defense and Scanlon watched the monkey on his team go higher and higher. He didn't worry about a fall, as he never sent a trained marine to a duty that the man couldn't perform.

Scanlon depended on the two men behind him to warn everyone if danger showed up, so he watched Thomlinson. He brought up his weapon to cover Thomlinson. He didn't see anyone else up there on any of the swinging walkways, but he was trained not to take chances.

He had gone through several assignments, and the last three were with this team, including Deeks. They had faced

the Trios and a group of arms dealers. He still needed to decide which group was the most awful.

This was the first time he had lost a member of his team,
and he had decided it was going to be the last. He scanned the
area in front and in back of Thomlinson. The climber was traveling like a fly on a wall. He was quiet and not making the
walkway swing. He blended in as much as possible, and
when he reached a point where Scanlon needed his weapon's
sight to watch his movements, he stopped.

Thomlinson's voice was a whisper in Scanlon's earbud.
"Loo, they are big naked males and are bipedal. I think they
are looking for something. They are tearing boxes apart with
their bare hands."

"Are they human?" Scanlon kept his eyes on the walkways
above.

"No, they have some type of outer bone structure over
their bodies in places. They have a blue tint to their body except for an orange-colored kind of point on the top front of
their heads that would almost be a horn. They have two eyes
and hard fins flaring out over their shoulders."

There was silence as Thomlinson moved his position.
"They have unusually long arms that must be strong, as they
are having no problem pulling the boxes apart.

They have scales that look tough, and if the shooter sent
bullets at them at three to four feet, it would hit them between
the groin and the belly. I have a feeling that is their only soft
spot. That makes them about eight-foot tall. But the bad news
is, if they lie down, the bullets would miss them."

"Do they have weapons?" Scanlon required the information.

"At this time, they don't. Something else, although they
have strong hands, there are no claws."

Scanlon thought this through. If the sarge was right and
this was a container of some type, then it might have been a

jail. If that was true, then the convicts were now free and taking over.

No one put harmless beings behind bars, so the ones that broke out could be very dangerous. Also, there had to be another breed out there that was fat like a slug and had claws. Now that was a picture to give you nightmares.

"Thomlinson, I want you to take care of yourself and don't give our position away. Still, I would like you to keep an eye on those blue guys."

"Aye, sir."

"Aero, Tumbler, we need to move forward to find that exit lock. Thomlinson has his sight on the aliens making the noise. From what he reports, we don't want to tangle with them. Aero, you have the schematic, and you probably have it memorized. You lead.

Tumbler, I need mid so I can check on Thomlinson. Ski, continue to update the ship. Take six."

"Affirmative." Three low voices answered together in Scanlon's earbud.

Going down behind the big equipment wasn't difficult, as they stayed in front of the piles against the outside wall. Whenever they reached a break in the cluster of boxes or piles, three marines would wait while one would carefully go down the rough aisle to the wall to examine the wall, looking to assure their location.

It seemed like hours and hours that Teve and Mags and been crawling through the tunnel used to flush air through the huge container. Actually, it had taken four hours with breaks and she thought the team had made the trip faster as they were used to moving in a bent position. She knew she was the one holding up the progress.

She decided she would just have to find a way to set a

better pace. She saw another arrow and as she twisted to look at the tube that was indicated, she was shocked.

"Teve, I need you to look at what we need to go through next." She flattened down on the floor of the vent and let Teve move above her to look at the smaller tube.

"Can you fit into that smaller opening?" She asked, looking sideways at him above her.

"Yes, it is a tight squeeze. I think that Scanlon and Thomlinson are big men with their extra equipment on, and if they could get through here, then I can with nothing but a blanket. Perhaps it would be better if I lead. You might feel better seeing me as something to keep your eyes on and move towards."

Oh my God, claustrophobia. She thought that word as she let him crawl over her to start into the small tube. She hadn't thought that she might have such a problem. She had never been in a situation that would cause her any such distress.

She had a hesitation as she got down on her stomach to follow Teve's bare feet. She was wiggling from side to side, pushing her weapon in front and pulling her pack behind, between her legs, before she realized she wasn't concerned about the tight quarters.

Mags concentrated on the big body in front of her as he swung from side to side like a cat on its belly. His muscles in his back and legs were moving him forward at a smooth even pace even in this tight round tube.

How could she have had any doubts that she could slither through this faintly glowing tube, following Teve? The movements were almost relaxing and watching Teve's feet was almost fun.

The movements were taking the tension out of her body that had built up for so many hours. She hated to stop when Teve said they should take a break. Mags went on ahead and drank some vitamin-infused water from what they had picked up from a pile left for them by the team. She was relieved to see Teve also drink.

Comfortable hours later, Teve whispered to the sergeant that they had a choice.

"Teve, are there any arrows?"

"Yes, I see the arrow and note now. It looks like we go into a big vent now."

"Well, I want to join the team. If they found a way to get to our ship or they have found something interesting, we need to join them as soon as possible."

Teve moved forward and pulled himself into the larger square metal vent. Mags joined him and could feel air flowing past them in this larger area.

She smoothed her hand over the metal by her shoulder. "Funny, this is almost like the tin or aluminum we use to build air vents in large buildings on Earth."

"It seems different from anything we have seen in this place." He ran a large hand over seams. When he moved it, there was a buckling sound under his foot.

"Careful, I don't think this thing was built for people to travel within it and you might find a quick way down to whatever is below."

Teve nodded and spread his feet out as he bent over at the hips to move forward. He tried to step on seams only, hoping they were stronger to hold the size of his body.

Mags pointed at the arrows and they moved on, using a bright flashlight until they came to a circle with a line through it. She looked at the arrows and instructions written around the scarred marks on the floor of the vent ahead of them.

"Okay, Teve, I think this is where we get out and try to find a way down to the floor. Thomlinson left us some of his special climbing rope, so I assume when we get this vent broken open, we will find we are above the floor."

She looked at the area that had been cut on three sides.

There was also the crumpled look to the fourth side that showed it had been bent open and then closed.

"I will have to try one of my knives to break through the seal the team used and bend this piece back." While she hunted for a sharp enough knife, Teve leaned over and just slammed a hand on the metal.

It buckled and dropped, hanging only on the one side.

Mags looked at the metal. "Or we could use your strength and that would work."

Looking around, she saw where the climbing rope could be fastened. The problem she saw was that she couldn't figure out how they were going to close the vent back the way the team had and fixed the metal.

"Teve, we have a problem. I'm not sure why, but the team wanted this vent closed up for some reason. I don't have the sealant that they used when they put it back in place."

Teve lowered his body and had his head below the opening. "I have an idea. There is a place where I can hang the climbing wire outside. You can climb down first and I will go out and bend the metal back in place before coming down the wire. How much mending tape and spray do you have in your med kits?"

While Mags sorted through her med kits and pockets, Teve was hanging halfway out of the metal vent. He put the climbing wire or rope, whatever it was called, around a large bolt several times. He didn't tie it, he just made sure he caught the loose end under the wrapped piece and pulled. It held, so he was ready.

"Sarge, can you tie all of that stuff into something I can hook on my blanket?"

Looking over at him, she had to smile. He was barely covered by a blanket tied like a college kid's toga. She pulled her backpack forward and searched through a side pocket. Coming out with a clean white sock, she put everything in it that

Teve needed.

Looking at it, Teve smiled. "Your feet are small."

Shrugging, Mags handed over the sock. "Well, for an Earth woman, my feet are big. They are a size nine. Also, the material stretches."

Teve pulled the top to a long length and tied it to his blanket. "Okay, use your rappelling skills and get down the rope. Do you have gloves?"

Sitting with her legs hanging over the opening, Mags took the time to put on her shooting gloves. They were leather with the finger ends cut off. Suddenly Teve had his hand around her neck and he licked her cheek in the way of his people.

She looked at those beautiful blue-green eyes and put her mouth to his in the way of her people. The kiss was warm, as he had learned fast. When their lips parted, she licked his cheek.

It was time for her to slide down the rope as she had been trained. The metal rope was a little short of her destination. It was near the floor, so she dropped off the end of the rope, tucked, and rolled. Her impact knocked her breath away, but as she waited only a moment to sit up, she found she had received no injuries.

Bringing her weapon around onto her chest, she looked up to watch Teve close the piece of metal with one hand. He had the wire wrapped around his leg and held onto it with one hand.

From her angle, she was watching an acrobat who was all strong muscles performing the impossible. He had been so gentle to her in the panic room that she had forgotten how strong he was, even in this form.

He got the metal back in place and taped it along with spraying it with all the things from her medical kit. It was an ugly, obvious patch, but the vent was closed. If the check was for looks, it would be caught, if the check was for integrity, the vent was again airtight.

Teve came halfway down the climbing wire. He stopped and seemed to jump up with the wire. The wire came unwrapped from the bolt and they both came down to the floor.

Landing with almost no sound, Teve hit the floor with one knee down and one foot as he kneeled to take the consequence of his fall. His body was made for this activity and he looked over her with a smile as the wire dropped beside him in a bundle.

"You know, Sarge, I could have turned and taken you down with me. I could have sheltered you from harm as I did before."

Remembering the fall through the floor with the debris, Mags also thought of their bodies together in the panic room. *Damn.* Was she going to get past that one time together with this big guy?

She jerked around with the MA12 up and ready to find a target when they heard the distant noise.

"Is that our team?" Teve was hunched into an attack mode.

Mags took a hand away from her weapon and touched behind her ear. "Hello team one. This is Sergeant Bloom. Can anyone hear me?"

She got an immediate answer from Ski, who was always handling communications.

"Hello Sarge, position?"

"Aero, we just hit the floor from the air vent. Your position?"

There was a pause, and Mags figured the team was talking things over about what to do next and what instructions to give to Mags.

"Sarge, we are about four hours ahead of you on the same floor. There are serious hostiles here. There is an exit lock on the outer bulkhead that our skip ship can put a suck tunnel on, but we have to find it first."

She relayed this information to Teve and then reported back to Aero.

"Affirmative. We will head your way with great care."

CHAPTER TWENTY-EIGHT

Thomlinson's voice was a whisper in Scanlon's earbud. "They have found something. It doesn't look like weapons. They are putting something on their bodies. It is the same color as their bodies, almost a metallic blue item. Oh, fuck."

Scanlon tensed, but he didn't say anything. He waited for Thomlinson to finish his report.

Finally, Thomlinson's whisper was back. "Lieutenant, what they put on is something that covers them tightly from their waist to the bend in their upper leg. It covers the groin area and had a special piece that would cover a penis on a man. This is armor that would protect them from the bullets from the rolling shooters."

"Affirmative. Do they look protected from our bullets all over their bodies?"

"With the heavy center section covered and with overlapping bulky scales and a thick skin, I think they are pretty tough. They seem to come with their own battle armor."

"Thomlinson, ease back. I don't want you to be seen by them. We are not sure about their eyesight, hearing or even smell." Scanlon's voice was low but stern.

He turned to look at his men around him. He motioned Aero over. "Any idea how close we might be to that exit lock?"

"Sorry. The schematic we saw upstairs was not great in details or dimensions, and this vessel is huge. We could be within ten feet or it could be hundreds of feet away. The skip ship has located it from the outside, but that's no help to us."

Scanlon frowned. "Okay, we have done this the hard way before, so let's get going." He was interrupted.

"Affirmative, Thomlinson, what ya' got?"

"Sir, some of the blue men have separated and moved off. I think that the direction they are going will put them behind you guys."

"Stay put. We need to find the exit." Scanlon told his men to be alert. They had reached another crooked passage to the bulkhead, and Aero left the point to go down to check behind the piles.

All Scanlon could think about was that this was going to be a long and hard trek.

For the first time, Mags relaxed. They were on a solid floor, somewhere near an exit. Their team was only a few hours ahead of them in this storage area and she was in the company of a shape shifter that she trusted.

Thinking about that problem, she realized she had never been afraid of the idea of shape shifters. The problem had been of something in a human shape that could change. As a scientist, she'd first said it was impossible.

Later, when she found out that it really happened, was documented, and she had taken the time to see the vids, she had to accept the fact. Inside, she still felt it was drastically wrong. She also found that a shifter often turned into something larger than their original form.

As a scientist, she decided this meant that they either absorbed additional body building material or their own material enlarged during the shifting process. That just wasn't right, and it infuriated her sense of calm and neatness in the universe.

Spending hours in a metal box having great sex with a shifter was not part of her universe either. Thank every God that people prayed to that it had happened.

Teve was leading the way between a large piece of machinery and a pile of misshapen items stacked too high for her to see the top against the outside wall.

Mags was walking with her head tilted up to look at the top of the pile when something blue swung out and wrapped around her body. Something big and warm was over her entire face, pressing her head back against a hard surface.

She knew immediately that something or someone had picked her up and was moving in long strides. She heard a loud roar behind and then the lack of air turned her world black.

Teve was several feet ahead of the female when he had the feeling of being watched. It was a normal reaction passed down by heritage from those who had spent centuries on a planet of jungles and predators. Being a warrior, the sense was strong in him.

Even in these modern times, the belief among his people was to keep and respect the heritage of their home life. They accepted modern conveniences without changing their world or their own feelings. He felt the eyes on him and turned to warn the sergeant.

He understood now what being in the modern world had done to his natural instincts. He was seconds too late in modifying his body. In another time, in an ancient age, he would have modified his body to protect those who needed protection.

Now he allowed the change to happen, but it was a minute too late as he saw a large blue beast's back disappear with the female of his choice.

To modify his body was as natural as breathing. There was the thought and there was the belief and there was the strength of the different body. He was now ready for war. It was just in time as another large blue figure stepped forward to prevent him from following his female.

This large blue being had plenty of strength and heavy skin as it took a defense position. It stood before him, its long arms raised. It had no weapons, but it was used to fighting with a large, invincible body. Now was the time to let this blue figure meet a better body with a mind that knew how to think as well as fight.

They both only took two side steps and then a long blue arm swung out. It was a mistake, and the only one the blue being would make, as it exposed the tender area under that raised limb.

The blue being was strong and had a longer reach, but a modified Veldan had claws, and it was with these that he took a large part of the chest away. The damage started under the arm and tore away part of the cartilage that covered the ribs and lungs.

There was a loud scream from the blue being as it turned around, automatically clutching at its death-dealing injury. It slowly sank to the floor, jerking and spreading a dark blue and red stain from its lifeblood draining from its body.

Teve didn't wait to see the final agony of the being as he moved over it and proceeded after his sergeant.

Aero called Scanlon over so he could speak quietly. "Lieutenant, the sergeant tried to tell me something and then got cut off. I think they're in trouble."

At that moment, Thomlinson spoke in Scanlon's earbud. "We have trouble. The blue men are splitting fast. They have moved around your location and are heading away from you. But I see a couple of new beings. Uglies. Bipedal, sort of. They are fat, even when standing, and have great ugly claws on their front legs. They don't look smart, but they look hungry."

Scanlon thought for a moment. "Fat enough that they would be taken out by the rolling shooters even if they lay down?"

"Affirmative."

"Marines, it looks like the insane have taken over the asylum. We have found the fat guys that the rolling shooters were made to take out, even if they lay down."

"Aero, let Ski work on tracing the sergeant. You concentrate on the exit lock. Ski, are we still in contact with the skip ship?"

"Aye, sir. They have reached the correct position. They have a portable tube ready. It won't keep us from the cold and lack of air, but it will allow us quickly to get from here to inside the ship's airlock. It will be tricky, but we all practiced for this except for the sergeant and Teve. We will just have to grab them and push them through."

Nodding, Scanlon thought about the problems he had right now for his team. They were separated from the sergeant and Teve, who were in trouble. They were threatened by some kind of hungry beasts that the builders of this ship had tried to keep corralled up and contained by rolling shooters. They needed to find an elusive exit lock in a maze of alien artifacts. *This is one great FUBAR.* With this thought, it was time to think of something positive.

CHAPTER TWENTY-NINE

M ags slowly woke as oxygen was allowed into her body. The hand covering her face had moved down to her shoulder, but the one around her waist was still tight. She didn't resist now, as she needed information for her foggy mind. She was slowly aware of her situation.

She now caught sight of a couple more beings traveling with them. They were as tall as Teve in his shifted form, but they were built different. They had very long arms and legs that seemed to have a deep scale covering.

She could feel some type of metal covering over the stomach and groin area of the being clutching her like a prize. Even in her full uniform, she felt the difference between the metal and what it protected. She wondered if she could get her weapon around enough to shoot it in the head above her shoulder.

When this creature had grabbed her, it had caught her with a long arm that trapped her arms against her body, holding her weapon against her below her breasts. Up to now, unless someone came up beside them, she had no way of moving the weapon to shoot at something.

She had gathered some information. There were three of the beings. They didn't have any weapons, and they seemed fairly intelligent. At last they stopped, and a being said something.

They looked at a pile of items that were stacked against the outer bulkhead, and one started climbing. When he got to the top, he threw down several small receptacles. One or two broke apart as they hit the floor, but several of the cases were metal and just bounced with a loud noise.

The one on the floor went for the metal items and, with the use of his unusually large hands that had four equal digits, tore them apart. He pulled out something that looked like a gauntlet.

The one holding her relaxed his grip, changing his arm lower. It released her arms and without hesitation she told the MA12 to fire at the being on the floor next to the open case.

Her deadly weapon shot true as always. The being's head exploded. The one holding her dropped her to the floor to turn. He was probably checking to see who was behind them to shoot at his partner.

What was behind him was Teve, in beast form — as large as the blue being who had turned to face him. Without stopping, both the blue being and Teve attacked, turning into a blur of two bodies.

Mags was still staring at the two fighters when again she was picked up from behind. This one was moving quietly backward. She resisted the urge to scream, not wanting to take Teve's mind off the being he was fighting.

She would let this one take her until she was positioned to have the MA12 kill it. Then she would come back and help Teve kill his adversary.

Suddenly, the alien holding her turned and began taking long steps that moved them away from the outside wall. They were moving quickly between the large machinery. She had a bad feeling that this blue guy knew where he was heading, and it wasn't toward the exit lock.

Teve's long steps were getting uncomfortable for Mags. She had decided she was tired of someone picking her up. Okay, as a woman she was on the tall side, but as a marine, she was on the small side. Among all those not from Earth, she seemed to be tiny. She was ready to use her weapon, but the guy had to set her down.

This being that was holding her was dodging and moving between the machinery. He was holding her so tight that her weapon was pressing into her ribs, restricting her breathing. His final turn was to duck into a blue, dimly lit hallway. At the end of it, she saw steps.

Okay, she had to do something to prevent him from taking her away from this floor level.

There were a couple of things the team learned immediately upon facing one of the fat clawed animals. First, these things were insane hungry animals, and second, they were hard to kill.

It came after them on all fours, sniffing with its wide, short nose, its pale eyes darting from side to side. Its long barbed tail whipped from side to side and it rose often on its strong back legs. Its fat stomach drooped down as it moved with its jaw open, showing the layers of sharp teeth.

The skin was an oily brown to black in the creases, or where light hit it. When it got a smell of them, it simply charged, long claws stretched out.

The first few bullets just sank into it. It had reached Ski as someone drilled holes into its head and it didn't slow down. It was a reflex of Ski sending several shots into its fat belly that stopped it and had it curling up and even tucking its barbed tail around it as the body shook and lay still on the floor. The black stain of its body juices slowly poured over the metal floor to Ski's boots.

"Lieutenant, he died when I shot him in that big fat belly." Ski took a step back from the big ugly varmint.

Scanlon nodded. "This is what the rolling shooters were built to take down. Even stooping over, its center is exposed. If it has a brain, it is in that fat middle area."

Aero, more used to aliens, added his knowledge. "That could also be where the heart and important organs are located. A large rodent might not have much of a brain stored in the head. Just enough to tell it to find food."

Ski looked around. "So it is closer to a cockroach than a rat. That means there are others."

"Yep, and they are worse than the blue aliens. These fat bugs don't think — they kill and eat. As far as we can tell, there aren't any rolling shooters down here." Scanlon looked around as he spoke through his earbud so Thomlinson would hear him. "Now it sounds like Teve and the sarge are in trouble with the blue aliens. And we still need to find the exit lock.

If and when we are sure we can get onto our ship, we will re-think what to do about our two missing teammates. Now let's move out and listen for the top guy to warn us about hostiles."

Their movement was slower as they worked forward on full alert. They came to another aisle to the outer bulkhead, but just as Aero went between the stacks, there was a call to halt.

Thomlinson spoke quietly through the earbud. "There is a fat one on top of the pile next to you guys. He will jump on the first one who goes toward the outer wall."

Aero whispered to the lieutenant. "If I take a step forward, it will scramble down those containers. You guys better be good shots at that big belly."

Not waiting for acknowledgement, Aero took a few slow steps forward. He was right in a wrong way. Hunger drew the fat animal down, but not in a slow scramble down containers. Instead, it jumped down, its claws out and the barbed tail sailing behind.

Because of the quick actions of the trained marines, just before it struck Aero, shots rang out, and its belly was torn apart. It was knocked aside, another body lying in front of Aero.

"Going in." These were Aero's only words. He stepped around the greasy body and went to the wall. He placed his hand on it and leaned in to look behind the stacks to see nothing but more flat walls with no warnings and nothing that suggested the exit.

Just as he was about to turn away, he caught sight of a bulge in the wall about fifty feet beyond this pile.

"Lieutenant, I think I see something about an eighth of a klick ahead."

Scanlon looked around for more aliens. "Affirmative Aero. Let's check it out and see if it's our exit lock."

It took them forty-five minutes and the kill of another cockroach before they reached a wide aisle that had an obvious exit lock. It had a red and blue light over it and several pads with holes in the wall around the thicker supports.

CHAPTER THIRTY

Teve fought hard against an enemy that was as strong as he was but had better armor. It was just a waiting game for Teve to keep his anger in check and his need for his female in abate. He would wait until the long arms swung the wrong way, and he used his claws on that weak point.

It changed this time, as the alien got tired and kicked out with the long leg with the strange foot that was almost like its hands. Even though it had metal armor at its groin area, as Teve ducked the kick, there was that soft spot where the armor met the upper leg, and he swung his claws.

The leg almost came off as Teve's claws hooked when he turned in his motion of attack. The alien went down on its back with its leg useless and liquid pouring from its body.

Teve did the *coup de grâce* and stamped down hard with his large foot onto the being's neck as it clutched at its leg. He heard bone and carapace crack and the alien no longer moved.

He had a few new bruises, but no scratches, as this enemy had no claws. It was a strong warrior and had fought a brave battle. Now he had to find the sergeant.

There was an idea running through his head as fast as his feet were running on the metal plates of the floor. The female looked different from the blue aliens. She looked a lot like the skeletons on the control room floor, except she was much smaller.

It was possible the being that took her might think she was one of several owners or builders of this container. If they thought they had captured a builder, they might also think they could make that individual take them somewhere that was important to them. Like their home world?

The good part of that was that they probably wouldn't kill her. The bad part was that they wouldn't let her go and might even torture her when she didn't do what they expected.

As an Earth female, her body was very fragile. She could easily die from abuse that they didn't realize they inflicted. He had to get to her now.

In his modified form, his sense of smell was powerful. He separated the odors as he moved between the aisles and found hers. He had to backtrack, as the one holding her had turned and gone down between the machinery. They were going away from the outer bulkhead.

He needed to hurry, but it was important that he not lose the scent he was following, so he carefully went between the equipment.

The trail turned and changed, like following a maze past the enormous equipment. Within her aroma, he caught her fear, but he also savored her anger. It was good that she felt anger, as it meant that she was awake and breathing. She could plan action if she was angry.

He maneuvered around another piece of equipment that reached above the wire walkways hanging high above most of the items. At last, a long hall that was metal faced him, dimly lit with blue light. Taking a moment, he made sure that she had been taken down this enclosure, then he stalked down it, finally seeing the steps at the end.

He was taking the stairs three at a time with his long legs when he heard a gunshot. It echoed down through the stairway, and he couldn't tell how far up the stairs it might have been set off.

He stopped and slowly went up the steps with his hands on the upper ones and his feet following. That could be the special gun that belonged to his female, and she could have fired it at her abductor. It was also possible that the alien got his hands on the weapon and fired it in some normal manner.

Worse, there might be other weapons available, or they could have moved out into a room where the rolling shooters were firing.

Suddenly he heard the loud noise of a klaxon alarm that resounded everywhere. Teve could hear it behind him in the large equipment room, rolling with echoes down the stairway and coming from above. It was so loud that it seemed to cause the metal walls to vibrate.

Thomlinson had come down from his high perch and the four marines were circling with their backs to Aero as he talked to the skip ship.

Aero felt he had confirmed with the skip ship that they were in the right spot. He was told that the ship was putting up the tube, which would only be about four feet long, to connect this exit lock to the ship.

After several moments of conversation, Aero heard a rap on the wall above the door. The little ship had found the right spot and was now hooked up. They had one man, the co-pilot, on the outside in an off-ship suit, just in case the tube had a problem.

Looking at the different panels with holes, there was one that was right next to the door and at shoulder height. Aero made the determination that these holes would be the ones that would open this door.

"Okay, while you guys have my back, let me explain what is about to happen." Aero talked out loud, not bothering with the earbud. "There is no airlock here for us. That means when I get this door open, the air from this room will blow anything standing close to the door outside. If our pilot has done their job correctly, we will be blown through the tube and into the back airlock of the ship.

We will have to hold our breath as the ship closes their door and brings their airlock up to atmosphere. The co-pilot can recover the tube and join the ship."

Scanlon listened as he watched for any more fat hostiles. "Suggestions, Aero?"

Aero had already put his weapon on safety and against his chest. "I think we need to be careful with weapons and move in close so we all go together. I will do a standard countdown, and then we say a prayer."

Scanlon gave the order to back up and for Aero to go when ready.

Aero took a deep breath, counted down from four, and at two he swiped the holes. The light above turned red on both sides, blanking out the green. A siren screamed in what sounded like a klaxon, hurting his ears as it echoed through the equipment behind them.

Aero watched the door move only a fraction and seem to hesitate. He had just about decided that it would not open when the door flipped sideways into the bulkhead wall. Instantly, he was pulled forward and felt the bodies behind him push against him as they were forced past the doorframe.

Before they reached the short trip to be inside of the ship, all movement stopped as the door behind them slid shut. There was a brief movement back toward the closed door, and then Scanlon did something unusual. He fired his weapon, and they were all pushed again to the open end of the skip ship.

Aero grabbed the first thing he could reach and, without gravity, pulled himself into the opening. Holding his breath, he grasped at any marine floating in and they reached out for another. At last, still within the deadliest environment for life, the back of the ship closed.

Just when Scanlon thought he was going to lose his entire team, precious air was creating a white fog in the freezing zone around them. The pilot slowly brought gravity to their position, and they sank down, sucking in the life-giving oxygen rich air flowing around them.

Too exhausted to do anything but lie on their backs and give thanks for the fact they were alive, they slowly breathed. Their rest was interrupted by an announcement from the pilot.

"Okay Marines, if you can move, I would like to get my copilot on board and get you over to the big ship to get you guys checked out."

Scanlon got everyone up and buckled in.

Thomlinson spoke first. "So, Boss, what next?"

Looking at all four sets of eyes that were looking at him, he gave a crooked smile. "Just what you expect. We get a group of gung-ho guys and fill them in on what to expect as we come back to this ship or container.

We need to pick up our two teammates and retrieve a body of a friend. No one left behind. If a couple of experts want to look this thing over after we come back from that run, we will make a detailed report."

Four voices rang out. "Aye, Aye, sir."

Teve was climbing the stairs but taking it with caution. He tried to fight his own need to fly upward and just attack. It was part of the warrior in this form—protect the female and kill the enemy.

What bothered him was that he heard nothing. He still had the sergeant's scent. It was intermixed with the alien that was carrying her. The alien's scent was new to him, so he had no way to determine if there were emotions hidden there that he could read.

At last, all the red lights had quit flashing and the sirens were done echoing throughout the building, Teve was also searching for additional sounds.

There was nothing. Either the blue alien carrying the sergeant had stopped moving or they'd entered a room. The stairway turned back on itself, and he was on the third tier when it was a good thing he was down on all fours.

A crude trap had been set to hit him in the chest and higher. Several boards and containers were set on a step, with one sticking out at the bottom.

If he'd been standing up, his knee would hit the board and the pile would quickly swing out, hitting the chest and head of the being on the steps. With a blow to the chest or head and all the items tumbling down upon them, the person would be thrown backwards down the stairs.

Instead, he bumped it with a shoulder, flattened against the steps, and let all the junk roll over him. After the clatter and noise quit, he slowly raised his head to make sure the path was clean.

So now there were two aliens. There was one that still had his female, and one to help take out the threat that was following. He let his claws grow long, both on his hands and feet. His teeth were ready to tear into anything, even thick scales.

Teve dug in and jumped to the ceiling, catching a grip on a panel that he tore off. He followed above the ceiling. They could set all the traps they wanted on the steps. He would follow her scent above in the dark as he moved over the ceiling.

This time, when he heard the gunshot, he didn't stop or hesitate. He just continued upward, finding the smell of cordite added to her scent, making it easier to home in on her location.

When he reached a place where the ceiling leveled out over

what had to be a room below, he knew he had found her. Her scent was strong, and there was a small bullet hole in the panel that allowed light from below shining through. She had shot her weapon upwards.

He took only a moment to confirm that there were two aliens with her. Good odds for a beast as angry as he was in such a killing rage. He should count to three, but at two he put all his heavy weight in a jump on one panel that let him fall through to the floor, facing one alien trying to force a door to close.

In this anger stage that he had been taught since a child to control, he let go and sliced the alien at the door. His longer claws went through the blue alien as if there was no scale or armor on the being. Before it screamed, it was dead, with body juices splattering everywhere.

He turned to growl at the one who was holding his female. This was the one sight that could stop an unleashed warrior beast in its tracks.

Sergeant Bloom was smiling at him as she was held in the arms of an alien. The smile was because the alien just didn't know what to do with her. It had her trapped in its arms, holding her against its body as she squirmed to move the gun around.

The problem was obvious. He couldn't let go of her because she would shoot him, and he couldn't hold on to her as she was swinging the gun around, trying to get it to aim at him somehow.

Teve saw a lot of blood coming from one leg where she'd wounded the being. Just as he stood in wonderment, her gun went off again, just grazing the head of the blue alien holding her.

He almost dropped her—or had he meant to toss her away? He had both arms around her, trying to keep her body tight and the wicked weapon against her chest. She was kicking and knocking her head back and doing whatever it would take to move her body.

Teve was trying to decide what he should do with this strange tableau in front of him. He looked at the large dark eyes of the blue being but could read nothing.

The sergeant was short in the tall alien's clutches, so its head was above hers and her feet were dangling well above the floor. With his great speed, he ducked, rolled forward and attacked the large, unusual feet of this being.

Immediately understanding Teve's move, Mags pulled her knees up, and with that much room, Teve knocked the alien off its stance, backward and down to the floor. Its grip on Mags relaxed, and she was tossed aside, continuing to turn over several times before she halted.

Bringing her weapon up, she had nothing to shoot at, as Teve the Beast was in a wrestling match with the blue alien that had been holding her. They were moving so fast and changing positions so often that she was afraid to give the order to her weapon.

As suddenly as it had started, it was over. She saw the blue alien swing his arm in a blow that, if it collided with the Beast, would take his head off. Before she could think the weapon to shoot, the Beast had claws into the underarm of the alien and the rip of scales and hard armor skin could be heard where she stood.

The alien screamed and dropped backwards. Teve roared a cry of triumph and was hunched in the stance of an animal that had just taken out his opponent.

Chapter Thirty-One

It had been very difficult for Teve to modify to the other form. The last fight and letting loose his beast was the worst change he had ever endured. Now he was exhausted and both he and the sergeant needed to find the exit lock.

Taking their time and with her weapon up and ready, they slowly made their way down the steps. Teve had a serious problem as he followed the sergeant. Coming off the extreme warrior-killing mode, his testosterone level was high, and it was all he could do to keep from throwing his female to the floor.

He tried desperately to be civilized, but the sweat on his forehead and palms showed his inner war. For once, he was walking slower than the sergeant. They had reached the hallway with the blue lights.

Part way down the metal path, Mags turned to look at her companion.

"Teve, are you injured?" She took a step back towards him.

"It is better to have distance between us." Teve held his hands up and took his own step, only it was backwards.

Putting her weapon over her shoulder so it hung behind her shoulders, she looked at him. "Teve, let me help you. I have a couple of med kits."

Feeling her as she moved closer, he went down on one knee. "It is different. I am so sorry, I need you."

By this time, she was close enough that he reached out and pulled her to him. "This won't be gentle, my female."

Her only word was "Wow."

He had her on her back, on top of her weapon and backpack and everything else, and he tore at her bottom uniform with small claws, ripping clasps and closures apart.

Mags didn't resist. There was something exciting about having sex in a dim blue hallway with the winner of a death fight, especially since the winner turned out to be Teve. He had warned her it wouldn't be gentle, and with all their clothes bunched down tying their ankles together, it was an athletic feat.

When he entered her, it was with one deep thrust that shoved her back against her equipment. She wasn't sure, but she might have said another *wow* as he filled her deeper than he had achieved the first few times they made love. *Yes!* even in this unusual circumstance, she called it love and not just sex.

He felt her being pushed forward on the floor, so instinct had him place one hand on the floor above her and when the other was free, he put it on her shoulder to hold her in place. Being deep inside of her, he felt the last of the warrior killer beast slip away. He could call out his change when needed without fear of the killer getting out of control. He threw his hips forward three times and the female enclosing him suck to take the juice his body ejected.

He dropped down but was amazed to feel her insides reflexing as she also had an orgasm. He wasn't sure if she understood, but she was his female.

He stayed on that one arm, keeping his weight off her and reluctant to pull out, to cut off the warmth of their contact. But reality finally hit him and the need to protect his female was now the important thing, since his body was relieved.

Mags looked up into the blue-green eyes and smiled. She had been smiling a lot lately. He finally got up, and she took a few minutes to clean up with some pads from a med kit. Pulling her clothes into place, she was up, adjusting her weapon and ready to start towards the exit lock.

They made it as far as the end of the hallway when they saw the first ugly, fat, greasy-looking guy with long claws. Her reaction and knowledge sent her weapon to fire at his belly, and he went down.

In behind machinery could be seen the shapes of several of the fat vicious greasy aliens.

"Teve, we can't go forward. Any suggestions? I have a lot of ammo, but it is limited."

"Sergeant, can you climb?"

She laughed as she put her weapon over her back and found handholds on the machine. "Every time you ask something strange, it is because I have to do something that is physically hard." She had almost made it to the first swinging deck when the fat brutal aliens discovered her.

Teve was right beside her. The ugly strange animals tried to claw upward but had no success. When they fell back, others attacked the ones who didn't get up immediately. Dinnertime.

Finally, Teve used his greater strength to get up on the first swinging walkway deck and reached down to pull her beside him. They both took a moment to rest and watch the strange, unsettling tableau below.

CHAPTER THIRTY-TWO

Scanlon's first argument was to convince the Colonel that there were dangerous alien animals loose on the container and that it looked like the original builders had been killed off a long time ago.

He explained the immense unit was no place for scientists at this time until they could be assured they wouldn't be killed within five minutes of stepping back through that exit lock.

After he won that argument, his next fight was to convince them to send a larger troop of marines back in to rescue the sergeant and the consultant from Veld. He also wanted to retrieve the body of his teammate from the top floor.

For Scanlon, the wasted four hours of irritating discussions made him think of the dangers to his people still in that container. Then he really got angry as there was the hold up because everyone in the new boarding troop had to be brought up to speed.

His team got fed and were given new uniforms and fresh weapons except for Tumbler, who took the time to tear his long gun down and clean it, then carefully rebuild it with his own hands. Since they all now knew what they were up against, they had better scanners to see the two types of aliens, fat ones and tall blue ones.

All the marines were given spray bottles of sparkle glue that would show the invisible killer wire. They still had only the cleaning nets as the best way of first finding the wires, although some thought that if they just shot off a lot of the sparkle glue, they'd find the wires. There soon were a couple of marines with sparkles on their backs or sleeves. There was one marine who was having a med remove some sparkle glue from his forehead, along with his eyebrows.

This time it took two skip ships to move over to the container. They took a solid tunnel with them, and two men from the ships set up the tunnel. It attached firmly to the unit's exit door and a skip ship could back up to it and firmly hook to the other end of the tunnel. Now people could go back and forth without needing to put on off-ship suits.

The first ship had Scanlon's team, along with ten more marines. The sixteen marines included two females. The new people going to board the interior had been told what both the blue aliens and the fat ones looked like, but it didn't really prepare them for the real thing.

They all entered the skip ship's back airlock and waited while atmosphere was pumped into the tunnel. A green light came on, and they went weightless as they pulled themselves across to the door on the side of the foreign floating tube.

Aero looked around at his lieutenant. "Who goes first, sir?"

Scanlon looked around and pointed. "The kid without eyebrows."

There was a snicker as the kid pushed his way to the front. Scanlon looked around with a frown. "Whoever just made the snicker can be last. Did we mention the fat aliens tend to pick off the last guy in the bunch?"

There was silence as everyone shifted around, some trying to get up to be near the front. Aero swiped his hand down and watched the door slide open. He whispered to the kid beside him.

"Stay close. Remember what we told you. Fire at their bellies, because that is their weak area."

This time, Aero notices there were no sounds of the sirens. He decided this was probably because there was no loss of atmosphere.

The whole group made it into the well-lit area of the aisle that led out to where the large machinery sat on the floor. Scanlon was pleased that the first-time marines remembered their training and did not look at the boxes or machinery. They were watching for hostiles.

The fat greasy looking black monster knocked the third guy in the group backwards with blood streaming from deep gouges. The long nails on thin long fingers attached to the short arms just shot out and with one swipe tore through the marine's protective uniform.

The young man without eyebrows had a score to settle. He was a marine, with or without eyebrows. He turned and fired, using his weapon on automatic. He almost tore the large brute in half as the bullets hit and the fluids poured out, splattering everything behind the large alien.

The one thing everyone realized was that the alien beast was bigger that they looked on a floating vid in a conference room. Seeing an enemy on a small vid and finding one towering over you in a real-life situation could make you lose your lunch if your training didn't take over.

The young marine without eyebrows had good reflexes, and his training kept anyone else from being hurt. Scanlon kept his face from smiling at having made the right choice. A little nudge could often make a man stand straighter. Still, he had to call a halt to allow the medic to pull the injured man back through the tunnel.

While the entry troop was reforming, Teve and Sergeant Bloom had made it up to a walkway above a group of hungry beasts that were actually feeding on one of their own. One of the fat greasy guys had climbed several feet off the floor before it fell back.

"Why the hell would the beings that built this container bring something like that on board?" Mags asked.

"Perhaps there were others, and they were destroyed by these." Teve said as he urged her to move forward.

After taking only a few steps, Mags stopped again. "A collection ship. Take a few animals or unusual beings from different places or worlds. Could they have been building a zoo someplace? But this time, they captured the wrong beasts, and it all got out of control."

She moved on as Teve gently shoved at her to walk on the metal swinging bridge. "I tried reaching Aero with my implant, but no answer."

Teve touched her shoulder. "See the ladder on your right? If you can reach it, we can get to a higher walkway. It will let us go across in the direction of the outer bulkhead."

Mags glanced where he'd pointed. "I think I can make that if you steady me from behind. But once we get up on the other walkway, I need a break. I don't have your strength and that little extra bit of exercise you put me through was the final touch to take my system down."

Teve was thankful that his female was so responsive to his needs. She was a perfect fit for a warrior, and he knew the council would approve. He wondered if she would understand what was in store for her when they got to Veld.

It was easy to help her get to the ladder, and he followed her up to reach the long walkway above the machinery. They walked far enough to get out of sight of the feeding frenzy, then the sergeant stopped.

"I need a break." She sat down and removed her backpack and weapon, dug out a water bottle, and accepted a protein bar from Teve.

He kneeled down beside her, looking over the wires to scan the floor below.

After finishing her short meal and taking some tablets for energy, Mags lay back with her head on her backpack. She watched Teve's jaw work as he munched on something, looking around for trouble.

It was when she heard repeated shots awakening her that she realized she had actually fallen asleep. Her weapon responded but had no target as she sat up confused.

Teve waved at her to stay quiet. He pointed in the direction the noise had come from further down the bulkhead.

"Sorry I fell asleep. Okay, I am ready." Mags got up and shook the last dregs of her rest out of her head. "How long was I out?"

Teve shrugged his wide shoulders. "About seven hours."

Mags gasped and reached to stop the big man. "Damn, how could you let me sleep so long?" Her voice was louder than it should have been.

"You needed the rest."

"Damn, Teve, we needed to move and get out of here. Where did those weapon shots come from? Our team must be in trouble."

Teve started moving on the walkway. His natural balance allowed him to move with jungle grace down the wire base, but she had to hang onto the thin railing. There was one on each side that had connections down to the wire flooring and up to the ceiling or other areas of connections.

For the most part, the walkway was sturdy, but Teve's weight caused some movement. Mags refused to think about the slight sway, even though she grasped the railings as she ran.

This was crazy, and she realized she was in a panic. Then she stopped, holding a railing and taking deep breaths. What had she been taught? Panic was the killer. She knew the answer. *Control is in the mind, and the mind controls the body.* She repeated her mantra, and she was in control.

She had her weapon up and spoke. "Teve, let me lead. I have a better weapon than your amazing body."

He stopped, giving her a long careful scrutiny, then finally nodded and stepped aside to allow her to move ahead.

She was moving smoothly and feeling sure of herself when she heard a barrage of weapons going off in the distance. This time, it was a little closer. She stopped, looked at Teve, and touched her neck behind her ear to activate her implant.

At the wide section beyond the entrance to the strange vessel, the marines had taken a closed vee formation. They were shooting with full rounds on automatic at the large animals that were attacking.

The animals were not smart and stood upright to slash with their front claws. This exposed their bellies, the one place they could be killed. This time, the marines were destroying the animals before they could get close, and no one was injured.

There were about twenty of the fat ugly brutes who just tore over each other to reach the marines. When the shooting stopped, there were some greasy black monsters injured, but still alive. They were actually eating on one of their own.

A couple of marines stepped forward and cut loose on the hungry uglies. Being cautious and stepping around the pile of animals they had killed, a marine had to ask a question.

"Lieutenant, what the hell are these things?"

"Don't know, Marine. We'll let the scientists figure them out once we find our teammates." Scanlon looked around, and suddenly Aero caught his attention.

"Aero, can you hear me?" the sergeant said through Aero's earbud.

Waving over his superior, he answered. "Praise my ass, Sergeant, it's good to hear your voice. Where are you? We have a full team to come and bring you home."

They all heard the sergeant's gentle laugh. "Look up and left. You are so pretty."

As Aero turned and looked up, Scanlon followed the same movement. Several yards away on one of the high swinging metal walkways were his two missing teammates.

CHAPTER THIRTY-THREE

Teve and Sergeant Bloom were back on the big ship, and there was a debate in the medical department as which of the two was giving the medics the most problems.

The medics had decided they had never heard so many negatives since they'd had to take a bullet from an Admiral.

Mags knew she had more knowledge than they did and will not let some kids examine her and give an opinion. And she was well aware Teve was convinced they didn't have the knowledge to understand his breed from Veld and give an opinion.

Finally, a man dressed in the light blue of the medical team but wearing the insignia of a major came into the cabin that held her and Teve. They were separated by the standard pull curtain that had been used in hospital wards for hundreds of years to give a small amount of privacy between medical beds.

Mags looked up with relief. "Thank goodness. Major, would you please tell these two medics that I am capable of understanding my own body and that I can be released right now?"

Teve yanked back the curtain and frowned, nodding agreement.

The senior doctor studied the floating charts on the wall. He looked at the sergeant and then at the big man from the planet Veld.

"You both have been through a lot and exposed to some strange virus or bacteria. You are covered in bruises and have possible internal damage." He looked over at the two medics.

"If these two continue to resist help, I have two guards just outside this door. We will immediately put them under a light anesthetic, and then you can help them at your leisure. Do your jobs, medics."

With these words, the Major nodded his head at everyone and turned to leave the room.

Since there was no more resistance from their patients, the medics completed their jobs in expedited time. Injections were given, gauze was applied, internal views were taken, and both patients were poked and prodded and finally released. They were instructed to find some down time.

It began again for Sergeant Margaret Bloom.

"No thank you, Sir. I regret to say that it will be necessary for me to refuse the offer to compile my notes and return to Earth. I really need to go back to the container and study the beings that built that object."

Mags stood at attention studying the Colonel's dour expression. His frown continued as he shuffled a stack of papers, studied a few of them and finally lifted his gaze to Teve, standing beside her.

"What about you, Consultant Teve? Are you refusing to file a report and return to your home world?"

Teve stepped forward, towering over the marines in the room. "No, sir. I feel it is time to return home. I worry about our mutual enemy. That is a constant threat to all of us. Although there might be much for scientists to learn eventually from this large item floating here, I see no connection to the Wisoo world."

He hesitated and looked only at the Colonel. "I would like to invite Sergeant Bloom to accompany me to my planet on her way back to her own home world."

Even though she was at attention, she let her eyes slide sideways to sneak a glimpse of the tall man beside her. She didn't want to go to a jungle, and she didn't want to go to Earth. She wanted desperately to return to the unit floating beyond this ship. After all, she was a scientist with a need to discover. There was so much to be discovered in that container. No, she wasn't going back to Earth.

She kept saying that to herself as her honor guard helped her get on the skip ship that was about to take off.

The Colonel had instructed that she was to be placed on the first scheduled ship heading out, so now she was aboard that ship, sitting next to Teve.

Mags's pout was showing. She hadn't pouted since she was ten years old and learned it never got her anywhere. It wasn't getting her anywhere now, but she just felt like ignoring everyone and frowning with her lower lip extended. She was going home, but she didn't have to like the idea.

The pilot made an announcement, the grabber engine caught a thread, and instantly they were in another part of the universe. Mags felt sick and fought it, pushing back in her padded seat.

There was another announcement, and Teve got up. The back of the ship was busy as things were being loaded into a small skip ship.

"Sergeant, I would really like you to come with me. There is something special I need to introduce you to in my world. I'm not sure you will agree, but I hope you will forgive me."

Mags blinked in surprise that Teve had spoken to her. She should say something nice and a goodbye of some type. She was still angry at being sent home. It was at this point that she realized Teve had extended his hand.

Going to a planet that was half jungle and half desert wasn't her first choice. Going home to Earth wasn't her first choice. She looked at that large open hand and had one thought. *What the hell.*

"I hope I don't regret this." Standing up, she didn't take the proffered hand, but walked around Teve to head back to the small skip ship.

In the back of the big ship, she looked over at a worker and pointed at her bags. "Throw those two into the skip ship. I'm going to take a vacation."

The trip down through the atmosphere was smooth as the small skip ship dropped them on a flat plateau. The humid air, full of strange scents, hit like a wall as soon as the skip ship lowered its back ramp.

Watching Teve pick up both his bags and hers, Mags took off her jacket and tied it around her waist. This was not a world for heavy clothes. At the edge of the plateau was a group of people dressed in soft green wrap-around clothes.

A couple of men stepped forward and took the packs from Teve after saying a couple words and giving a short bow. They spoke in a language Mags didn't understand, and she needed to get her translator out of her backpack. Unfortunately, the backpack was disappearing over the edge of the plateau on the arm of a native.

Teve's long strides put him in the middle of the group of his own people, who were giving short bows and then all talking excitedly in their own tongue. She watched them all turn to go down off the plateau.

It took her only a moment to race across the flat ground and yell out at Teve. "I need my translator from my backpack. I don't speak your language."

Mags followed the group down the steep climb, slowly passing the tops of high trees and then getting into the blue green color of the ground below. This was all sheltered from the overgrowth, so rich and so heavy that only stray sunlight beams filtered through the limbs. Flowers, plants growing on other plants and leaves of every size and form filled in the world around her.

She stumbled on a root as she stared upward and looked around to see the natives far ahead. Taking a deep breath of the oxygen rich air, she tried to look down at the path closely so she could catch up with Teve and his friends without falling.

As she got close, she called to him again. "Teve, I need my backpack."

When he stopped to look at her, everyone else did the same, staring at her as if she were a strange bug. Teve walked back to her, speaking in English.

"I forgot. Sergeant, even your translator will not help with our local dialect. I also forgot you weren't used to our jungle. It would be easier on you if you were to shed some of your clothes." Teve pointed to the small amount of brown and green leather looking apparel that the others were wearing.

The sun over this planet shed a different spectrum of light, and Mags's eyes were still adjusting to the filtering color. The sky was not the same color blue as on Earth. It also meant that the colors of the jungle were different, as they seemed darker and deeper.

Mags looked at the others, who suddenly got interested in the fauna. "If you can convince your crew to wait a minute, I will get out of this uniform."

Sitting down on the ground, she undid the laces on the heavy boots and took them off. Next came the heavy uniform pants and, after looking around, she even took off the long underwear. This left her with the good standard marine shorts that they called female panties.

Mags stood up and unwrapped the tied shirt at her waist, took off the undershirt, and found that her military bra covered enough. Looking at several females, she saw that their the wraps barely tied over their nipples.

She was slipping the heavy boots back on when Teve held onto one to have her wait. He went to his crew, and a couple of people gave him pieces of leather-like material. He came back, stopped at a plant, and pulled off a couple of large leaves. Returning to her, he kneeled and picked up one of her feet, then wrapped a piece of leather around it. He took a leaf and stripped some strings from the back it. He took these strings to wrap around the leather and, pulling the leather up around her ankle, had a very neat foot cover.

As he repeated the process, she saw over his broad back the startled looks from his crew. Evidently, this was not a common practice for Teve or Veldan worriers to do for people. Or maybe it was because she was an off-world person.

Mags saw a strange look come over him as his eyes turned dark green. He turned away, leaving her alone. She gathered her clothes, tying everything into her jacket except her boots. She tied the shoelaces together and slung them over her shoulder. She hung onto her bundle with one hand and now felt able to move in this wet jungle.

She followed Teve and the people that came to meet him. There was very little talk, and it was in a language she still didn't understand. A man in front had her backpack along with other luggage. He was as tall as Teve, but the rest of the people were all a few inches shorter. They were all over six feet, but not as tall as Teve or the front guide.

So her guess was that the front guide was of the warrior breed, the same as Teve. Okay, maybe it was not a bad idea to spend some time on this planet. There was a lot to discover.

She had to admit being stripped down to her underwear was much more comfortable in this humid green world she was walking through, but she was glad none of the marines could see her at this moment. She heard noises in the trees and bushes and looked back when she saw something move out of the corner of her eye. This world was alive.

Because she wasn't looking, she stumbled again. This time she fell flat on her face, her weapon hitting her chest as she dropped to the rough, damp ground.

Teve was immediately there to pick her up and help her without a word. He picked up her bundle and handed it to her, but she saw some people frowning as they watched.

"Teve, your people are not happy that I am here, are they?"

"I am sorry, Sergeant. There are more involved here. We also are taking footpaths instead of using vehicles due to the Trios. They are on this side of the planet, hoping to catch another modifier to run tests on." He waved at the surrounding trees.

"Your own people have sent down another contingent of fighters to dig out these invaders. They have sent us back to our ancient times in order to elude them and keep our families safe while we get them out of this area.

My people are angry about a lot of things, but they aren't angry with you or you being here. Now, do you need help? It is important that we travel fast for a bit to get to a safe point with some of our elders."

CHAPTER THIRTY-FOUR

If she thought all the trouble and efforts on the container had stressed her body, this long trek through the jungle wore her out fast. Her logical mind said that the oxygen-rich air should help her body endure the long trudge through the green wall.

Although there was a misty gleam of sun showing streaks down through some breaks above, there was no sight of the sky. In the distance, Mags could hear the roar of something large, but the people she was traveling with didn't seem interested.

They stopped once for a food break. They shared their food with each other and Mags. She looked at each of the pieces handed to her and decided they were tubers of some type. The taste was good, and she had to use her teeth a little more than on the soft protein bars.

Water was in gourds that were passed around with no hesitation as everyone's lips touched the top to drink. Mags decided her shots would protect her, so when Teve took a long drink and handed her the vessel, she tipped it up and was surprised that the water was cool.

She would need to ask Teve later how the water stayed cool in the gourd. To relieve their bodies, everyone found a bush and squatted. This seemed barbaric to Mags, but she couldn't walk with a full bladder.

As she looked around in confusion for a suitable bush, Teve nudged her, and she found he was trying to tell her he wanted her to follow him. He stopped at a bush and handed her a couple of large leaves. She saw him turn his back on her as he took a large protective stance.

She decided it was now or never and never would be too uncomfortable. The back of the two leaves were fuzzy and soft and served better that the artificial wipes the military supplied. Not only that, Teve explained, you covered up your waste and left it for bugs and jungle growth.

Teve also explained you must hide it in a manner that the Trios would not discover. Mags smiled as she watched him move some jungle debris over her personnel debris. Now it was time to get back to their travels.

It was almost night when they reach what Mags would later call civilization. First the path became wide, then it turned into a paved road. Ahead, she saw lights, but they were aimed down to the ground so that they would not be seen from above. Whatever they shined down on did not reflect back.

Suddenly, two very large men—guards—stepped out to greet them. At first, Mags couldn't distinguish any buildings, just large hills of jungle. But as they got closer, she saw the doors and windows and realized that the hills were actually buildings.

These amazing people had allowed the jungle to grow right over the rock-hewn buildings. Her mind immediately put the system together. It preserved nature, hid them from the Trios and gave them natural climate control.

She knew they never had to worry about heating their buildings, but there would be the need to cool and dehumidify for comfort. Water and food could be worked into this natural environment with very little effect on the natural life of the jungle, and waste disposal would be handled through piping under the buildings.

She would have to find out how far away they pumped the waste. On the other hand, if they ate a lot of natural products, a lot of their cooking material might be fed back to animals or used as fertilizer for their food plants. It was a natural cycle that would work well in a population that was controlled.

She had a sad thought, knowing it wouldn't work on Earth as it was populated by a group of humans who had no self-control. *Too bad.*

Teve led her away from the people they had traveled with and kept stopping every so often to ask a question or speak to a passerby.

"Teve, what's the plan?" Mags looked into doorways and windows as they walked down a wide alley.

"I am hoping to find Sever and Charley."

"Ooh-kay, and should I know who Charley and the other guy might be?"

"Charley is an Earth woman who lives here with Sever. Sever is a modifier like me and was captured by the Trios. Charley helped him escape, and they have been together ever since."

Well, well. Teve's words stopped her in her tracks. Yes, this was a world she needed to look at more closely. She followed Teve down the covered alley. It was several stories high, with walls of buildings on each side. Looking up, she saw the alley covered by the growth of the jungle that had been allowed to expand over the buildings.

She wondered if the buildings had had been built from stone or carved out of a mountain of rock. It was dim, almost twilight in this alleyway. There were more lights here, as they would not be exposed to the upper sky or any ship.

"Teve. How many people live here?" She continued to look around as she followed him.

Teve turned another corner and then waited for her to catch up. "There are about thirty thousand at this location."

That information stopped her. She thought about the people and about the technology both her military and the Trios had that could pick up movements and heat signals.

"Why don't the Trios find a heat signal that large at this location?" She waved her hand at the large walls. "They will find traces of movement."

Teve pointed to a section that she couldn't see, high and in a different direction.

"There is a quiet volcano above us. We are over deep buried lava tubes. It is hard for a searcher to distinguish any heat registration. We also have tunnels for our people to travel out before going through the jungle paths. It is strange, but what we did to protect our planet from natural disaster has now turned out to protect us from off world enemies."

He turned and looked at the walls and lights, then up at the green roof. "This is our largest city. We prefer to have smaller cities and towns. We prefer to control population growth. Modifiers can only have two children in their lifetime. Unless . . ."

She looked at him in this cool place, seeing him in his rightful home. She thought about what he was telling her about his lifestyle and about his people. Two children to take the place of each parent, once those parents were no longer of this life.

Teve turned and pushed a door open, waiting for her to enter. She was waiting for him to finish his statement. Unless what? Since he was just waiting, she walked into the building and found herself inside a pleasant apartment.

It was a large open arrangement with minimal furniture. She saw the kitchen past a waist-high bar, and drapes moving in a breeze allowed views of a comfortable bedroom. She knew it was his home when she saw the display of antique weapons on two walls.

She looked around at the soft light glowing from a couple of inset stones in the walls. The floor was cool and covered in areas with woven rugs with interesting patterns of animals that she couldn't identify. Everything was blue and green like his eyes.

She finished her turning as she examined the apartment and was facing him behind the food bar as he stood in the kitchen area. "Wow, Teve."

He shrugged. "You should see my desert home."

"You have a desert home?" She walked towards him in amazement.

"No." He just leaned on the counter, looking back at her with those amazing jungle eyes.

Mags stopped. "Teve. You made a joke. I didn't even know you had a sense of humor. I only saw you smile once or twice, and it was a little smile. Wait, you never finished your sentence. You left off with the word unless."

Now she was surprised as Teve looked down at his hands on the counter. He cleared his throat and appeared to be hunting for something. He was hunting for words.

"Teve, have I created a problem by coming here to Veld?"

"No, I created a problem by bringing you here." He looked up at her. "What do your family or friends call you? I can't keep calling you *Sergeant*."

Now she was the one who needed to hunt for words. She wondered what she wanted him to call her. In that dark tight room on the container, he had whispered words in his own language that instinct told her were love words.

"My first name is Margaret, but friends call me Mags."

"Your people call your females strange names. I will call you Maggy. It suits you better for me." He smiled a real smile, and that worried her.

He didn't move from behind the counter that seemed to protect him. "*Unless* . . . unless we choose a life mate from a different world. Then we can only have one child to replace the one Veldan that will leave a place when they die."

Mags looked around the room and went to one of the large soft-looking seats that had had no sides or backs. They were more like tall long couches, about three feet high, with furs across them. She sat down on one and peeled off her weapon.

"Teve, I think you just proposed to me."

"I'm not sure what that means. I am asking you to stay at my side until whatever God or gods you believe in separates us."

Sitting there in shock, she finally was at a total loss for words. She could not remember a time in her life when she couldn't think of something to say. Her mouth had many times gotten her into trouble because she didn't keep her words from flowing out too much and too loudly.

She searched through her mind. "Teve, there is such a difference between us. You change into a beast to fight the Trios and I work in a modern laboratory to make weapons to help my military fight enemies. We are worlds apart."

He moved around the counter. "Come with me, sweet Maggy. I'm not handling this right."

He grabbed her hand and pulled her out of the apartment and back into the dim sweet-smelling alley. She didn't resist as they moved through the city, past large buildings with archway openings and people gathering inside.

She wanted to look and see this amazing city and all the people, but he was going as fast as she could go without being pulled off her feet.

They came to a point that opened up to a wide hallway with wide steps leading up that seemed to go inside the rock of the mountain. The deeper they went, the cooler the smooth walls and steps felt.

Finally, the steps stopped at a wide hallway, and there were now many people. These people, natives of Veld, were all dressed in long smocks of different colors.

CHAPTER THIRTY-FIVE

Teve opened a wide door and invited her to enter.

Mags's eyes went wide as she saw what any lab rat would recognize — a modern, well-lit, clean laboratory, spread out as far as she could see. She decided it was better than her old one on Earth. To begin with, there were no armed soldiers at doors checking entrants and exits.

There was something else that drew her into this developing place. There were no barriers. She could see sections that showed experiments on mechanics. She could identify glass enclosed chemical investigations, yet even though they were far away, anyone could see inside.

This was a lot of movement in many areas, and in some zones, it seemed to be almost chaos. In other sectors, with long tables full of equipment, there were only a couple of individuals barely moving.

Mags took a deep breath and walked forward. She forgot about Teve. She forgot about the container. She just took in the amazingly important modern place with a smell she knew from working in such a place on Earth.

As she was walking between long benches, a man grunted and the barked out a command. "Give me the crucible tongs." Mags looked around and realized she was the only person close to the tall man.

He had his hand out waiting as he was holding onto a flame control with the other. She looked at all the items on the bench, clean and new tools. Without hesitating, she picked up the tongs and slapped them firmly into his hands.

He said nothing else, as he used the unusual shape of the tongs to grasp the small volumetric flask that was over the flame. He seemed content and turned the flame down and removed the flask with the tongs.

Mags wandered on down the long line of benches, taking time to look into the glass enclosed chemical rooms. There was a lot of care being taken in those rooms, as the people were enclosed in self-contained clothing. She could see the safe lockers attached where they entered from another side. She could also see the double thick walls and glass or whatever the clear views were made from that was protection. There was no chance of danger escaping from those rooms.

At last she reached the rooms where clear baffles were set up to control the noise and smoke caused from machining metal. She moved close to a tall woman who was grinding a small part. There was an attachment on the grinder that sucked up the free metal parts and any smoke. The woman's bench was clean.

Mags fell in love with this place. She could have built her rocker weapon in half the time here that it had taken her through the red tape on Earth.

The woman said something to her in a language she didn't understand. It was at this point that she realized that the man out in front had asked her for the tongs in English. She looked around for Teve and he was leaning one hip against a bench a few feet behind her.

"They all know who I am, don't they?"

Teve nodded. "Some of them consider it an honor to have you in this laboratory."

Mags looked at the woman, who was smiling. "How do they know about me?"

There was a sigh from Teve. "It is your discovery on your weapon. You know why the rocker weapon won't work for everyone."

Turning to look at what the woman was building on the bench, Mags picked up a small piece of metal and then another and fit the two items together. The machining was so good and so precise that they were like one piece. Even with nothing to hold them together, they wanted to stay as one piece. Mags didn't know what the woman was making, but it was going to be perfect.

Like putting these pieces together, she figured the rest of it out. "My weapon only works when it is given into the hands of a soldier who believes inside himself that it will work when he asks it to work. That is why we discovered it had failed so many times. I believe Thomlinson could use one, but I don't think Tumbler would ever get one to shoot."

She turned to face those blue-green eyes in that tall, broad man. "That is why the Trios will never get the modifying gene to work for them. They will never understand the special trigger."

Teve gave a single nod and waited.

As a scientist, Mags knew what waiting was all about. If you were going for an answer, whether in a virus or a gene or in a tool, it didn't come immediately. It came with patience. It came with trial and error. Basically, it came with mistakes and trial and error. It also came with determination and intuition.

Mags just felt there was no problem with the rocker weapons. They worked for her and for a few people. She insisted it was just some soldiers that couldn't adapt to the weapons. The military didn't like to think that their trained personnel weren't acceptable, so they would not approve the weapon for mass production.

"The Trios will never discover your secret, no matter how long they process the genes they take from trapped modifiers. My God, they will keep this war going until you have no more people alive on this planet."

She turned to the tall woman. "We have to do something.

We have to find something that will drive those monsters away. It must be in such a manner that they will never come back, ever again."

Teve stood and walked right up to her. "Does that mean you are going to stay on Veld?"

Carefully laying down the two pieces, she looked at all the rest of the partially machined items. Finally, she turned to look up at his strong face.

"Of course I'm staying. I couldn't leave with the possibility of the Trios capturing someone I care as much as I do you. I have to figure out a way to get them off this world. I have to protect you."

"First, come back to my apartment. We need to talk this through and make sure we both understand what this is all about. We need to make sure we both agree to what the future holds for us together."

It was hard to leave this fantastic place that felt like the future. Teve explained she was seeing only a portion, and that there were two more floors in this location. He also told her there were three other sites that did different types of scientific studies.

For Maggy, as she now thought of herself, it was like being reborn. She was in a natural world that was not being harmed by the brilliant people that protected it.

Chapter Thirty-Six

M aggy lay in the large bed with her head cradled in the arm of what, at one time, she had termed a beast. She had a life shaking decision to make, and it needed to be made before she took the satellite call that had come through earlier.

The call had contained a warning that the Wisoosio were bringing in stronger forces. All foreigners to Veld were advised to evacuate as soon as possible. Large Earth ships bringing in troops would be available for only a short time to help with this withdrawal.

The incoming private call was to inform her where they would pick her up personally by a skip ship. If she told them she couldn't meet that appointment, she was committing herself to an agreement with Teve.

To stay on this planet and work in that great ultra-modern laboratory was not a difficult decision. To commit to a lifetime with an alien shifter was a whole different story.

It first involved changing her mind about shifters. She must access her true scientist and forget her bias. She had to accept that like her rocker weapon, a shifter was a natural part of nature.

So she had to erase that work and understand the word modifier. It was a determined thought of a special person to modify their body. Like her weapon, it was a change to protect that person and allow that person to protect others.

Moving to seek heat from the large body sleeping beside her, she was now comfortable, thinking of the miracle that thousands of years had taken in mutations to produce such a weapon for this world. Yes, now it felt right in her mind.

In a small way, on the back of the ship, he had tricked her into coming down to his world. When they returned to his apartment, he explained he had an emotion for her that his people called *drawn*.

She supposed on Earth it would be called love. Now she had to face what she felt for him. Could she be committed to a man who changed into a beast? Did she love a shifter? Last night, when he brought her to the peak of her orgasm and she screamed his name, she would say she had deep feelings for him.

She thought about what the enemy might do to him and his people. She knew in her heart that she could help the people on this planet.

Thinking of her heart, she became aware she didn't want to leave this beast. She couldn't bear the thought of being apart from him. She forgave him and she forgave herself.

She would ignore the call and the pickup appointment. She would stay in this jungle with this blue-green-eyed beast, and she would help the people of this planet in this war.

The End

ABOUT THE AUTHOR

The author lives in Florida and under the pen name of M. Garnet (Muriel Garnet Yantiss) spends all her time writing, reading or talking to writers and readers.

Writing SciFi, Fantasy and Adult Romance. Her web site is www.mgarnet.com to show all the books she has written. Find her on Amazon at her Author's site at: https://www.amazon.com/author/m.garnet

She loves to hear from you at mgarnet2@yahoo.com. She answers all emails.

Put in a word where you found this book to let others know how you liked this story. Thanks.

Books by M. Garnet

Scifi Novels
The Spacebinder and The Thousand and One Nights

Witch's Curse Series
Witch's Smoke Aaron
Witch's Moisture Breandon
Witch's Heat Cian
Witch's Cold Donal
Witch's Curse Collection

Lovers Curse Series
Lovers Knot of Four
Untie the Lover's Knot

Moore, Moor & More Investigators Series
There be Ghosts Here
A Hole in the Ground
The Vampire Cult Investigation
How do you Capture a Vampire

Stories In Contemporary Time (Stand Alone Novels)
Black Ghost Runner
Eyes of Danger
Falling to the Viking
Probing Shadows
The Midnight Queen
A Master Trade
Bloodline
The Younger Tea
A Voice in the Darkness

Holiday Stories (Stand Alone Novellas)
Trading Parties
Celebrate a Holiday Eve
Decorate my Palm Tree
The Future Nutcracker Prince

Stories By H. Beryl Series
Drawn In
Letter Training
Emergence is the Process
Midnight Black and Blue
Shadow of Doubt
A Xmas for Xo
Emergence of Heat & Crime

www.ingramcontent.com/pod-product-compliance
Lightning Source LLC
Chambersburg PA
CBHW051500170626
46811CB00002B/572